# Dog Willing
*a golden retriever mystery*

### Neil S. Plakcy

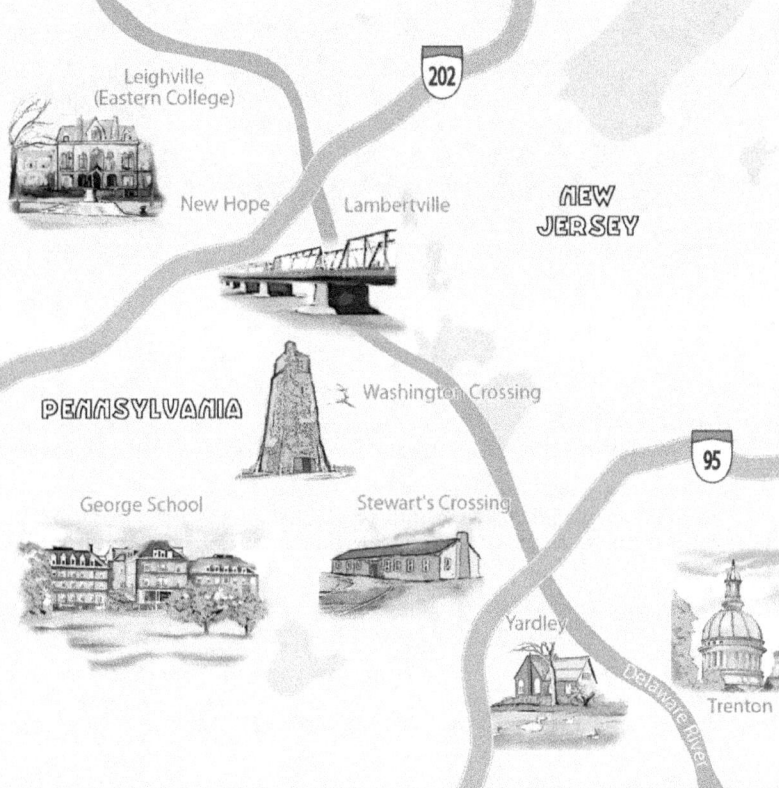

# Reviews

When his neighbor is accused of murder, reformed computer hacker Steve Levitan and his golden retriever Rochester are asked to sniff out clues to prove her innocence.

Who could have killed bookstore owner Darlene Nowak? One of the food truck vendors she angered when they parked in front of her store? Someone from the writer's critique group she sponsored? Steve knows that cooks and creative folks are very sensitive about criticism—but could one of them be angry enough to kill?

Mr. Plakcy did a terrific job in this cozy mystery. He has a smooth writing style that kept the story flowing evenly. The dialogue and descriptions were right on target.

*Book Blogger Red Adept*

Steve and Rochester become quite a team and Neil Plakcy is the kind of writer that I want to tell me this story. It's a fun read which will keep you turning pages very quickly.

*Amazon top 100 reviewer Amos Lassen*

*In Dog We Trust* is a very well-crafted mystery that kept me guessing up until Steve figured out where things were going.

*E-book addict reviews*

Neil Plakcy's golden retriever mysteries are supposed to be about former computer hacker Steve Levitan, but it is his golden retriever Rochester who is the real amateur sleuth in this delightful academic mystery. This is no talking dog book, though. Rochester doesn't need anything more than his wagging tail and doggy smile to win over readers and help solve crimes. I absolutely fell in love with this brilliant dog who digs up clues and points the silly humans towards the evidence.

– Christine Kling, author of *Circle of Bones*.

Copyright 2022 Neil S. Plakcy

This cozy mystery is a work of fiction. Names, characters, places, and incidents either are products of the author's imagination or are used fictitiously. Any resemblance to actual events or locales or persons, living or dead, is entirely coincidental.

All rights reserved, including the right of reproduction in whole or in part in any form.

# Chapter 1
## *One for the Books*

As soon as Rochester saw Emma across the dog park he took off. Theirs was a romance made in literature – the Brontë hero and the Austen heroine. It didn't matter that he was a golden retriever and she was a yellow lab, or that they'd both been neutered.

We had known Emma and her mom Arielle for several years by then. They lived a few blocks away from us in River Bend, our gated community at the edge of Stewart's Crossing, Pennsylvania. We often met up on our walks around the neighborhood or at the dog park.

It was the first warm day of spring, in early March, and yellow forsythia blossomed around the edges of the fenced-in square, with a batch of new buttercups at one corner. When I was a kid my friends and I used to pick them and rub them against our chins to see if we liked butter or not. Looking back it was an odd tradition, but then so was making wishes on dandelion seeds or picking daisy petals off to see if someone loved you.

I walked over to where Arielle stood with Emma's leash in her hands. She was in her late thirties, with a bob in her brown hair that made her look very French even though she had been born in the United States. Her look was complemented by thigh-high black boots, a black leather skirt, and a gray cashmere sweater over a white blouse.

"Hi, Steve," she said. "I see the romance between Emma and Rochester is as strong as ever."

She pointed to where Emma had rolled on her back and Rochester was licking her face. "Too bad his name isn't George Knightley."

"Or that hers isn't Jane Eyre," I parried back, sharing her love of English literature, even though I hadn't named Rochester myself. I had inherited the big golden retriever four years before, after the death of his previous owner, and though it hadn't been love at first sight between us, eventually he had become the main reason I'd come back to life after the end of my marriage and a year's stint in the California penal system for computer hacking.

I'd come a long way since then, and I was grateful for all the blessings in my life. The only real issue, if you want to call it that, was Rochester's nose for crime. Well, that and my own curiosity had dragged us into the investigation of several murders.

Arielle and I both laughed, and then she pulled a postcard from the pocket of her skirt and handed it to me.

"Food trucks?" I asked as I skimmed it.

"Pierre and I have finally broken up, and he moved out last month." I knew that Arielle was a stay at home mom of two kids, that she had gone to cooking school and that she and her husband were having problems.

"I'm sorry to hear that. I went through divorce myself, so I know how tough it can be."

"It's for the best. But I need to make a living myself, and I've opened a food truck. With two kids, I can't go back to the bruising routine of a restaurant kitchen, but I can manage the offbeat hours of the truck rallies."

"You'll be at the Stewart's Crossing Shopping Center on Saturday?" I asked, looking down at the card again. "I'll have to come by and sample your wares."

"That would be great. And then spread the word."

Rochester bounded up to me with a worn green tennis ball in his mouth. "You want me to throw the ball?" I asked. I tried to grab it from his mouth but he kept his jaws tight.

"How am I supposed to throw this if you won't let it go?"

Arielle was snorting with laughter at this point. "Emma does the same thing."

I finally wrested the ball from his mouth and threw it into the center of the dog park. He took off after it, caught it on the second bound, and then settled down on the grass with the ball in his mouth.

I shook my head. "I call him the Golden Thiever, because he's not interested in retrieving, just grabbing."

Arielle looked at her watch. "My kids will be home soon. I'd better get dinner cooking."

She called Emma, and that distracted Rochester from his ball. The two of them ran around for a while before running out of energy. Or so it seemed; once I had Rochester back on his leash for the walk home, he tugged and pulled as much as ever.

A wind picked up, and I shivered inside my lightweight jacket as Rochester nosed around the base of a leafless oak tree. "Come on, dog, these forty-six-year-old bones get cold too easily. Pick a spot and pop a squat."

He looked up at me, his black nose twitching as he sniffed the air. He was quite a handsome dog, his hair a rich gold that glowed in the light, with a square head and big brown eyes. When I looked up photos of the breed standard online, it was as if Rochester had posed for the pictures himself. He did his business and we hurried home as the sky turned shades of purple at the horizon and the chill set in.

We got home just as my sweetheart Lili was pulling into the driveway, and Rochester tried to charge forward as he had with Emma, but I kept a tight hold on his leash. Lili was carrying an armload of student portfolios and I didn't want him to knock into her and make her drop them.

I kissed her cheek as I held the door open for her. "Your lips are cold," she said.

"Cold lips, warm heart?" I asked with a smile. I thought for a moment of my father, who'd known a million clichés. What would he think of Lili? He'd always appreciated a beautiful woman, and with her curvaceous figure, flashing dark eyes and heart-shaped face, she radiated beauty. She also had a kindness that my ex-wife Mary lacked, that I was sure he'd have responded well to.

Lili and I both worked at Eastern College, a few miles upriver from Stewart's Crossing. I ran a conference center called Friar Lake, and she was the chair of the Fine Arts Department, and taught the occasional course in photography. "Midterm projects?" I asked, as she set the pile of portfolios down on the dining room table.

"No, everything in this semester's class is digital. These are submissions for an exhibit in the art gallery."

I began boiling the water for pasta for dinner. "Anything good?"

"I've had them on my desk for most of this week, and I haven't had a chance to look at them yet. I hope I'll have some time this weekend. You have anything planned?"

I told her about Arielle and her food truck as I poured the pasta into the boiling water. "I thought we might go over there Saturday for lunch."

"Sounds like a plan. I'm going to go upstairs and let my hair down. I'll be back in a few minutes."

Lili had a gorgeous mass of auburn curls which she kept pinned up during the week. While she went up to fluff them out and get out of her work clothes, I boiled the pasta, steamed broccoli florets, and chopped pine nuts and sun-dried tomatoes.

While I worked, I thought about my parents. I knew that they didn't care for Mary. But my mother had kept her mouth shut—I'd brought home a Jewish girl, after all, one who was smart and pretty, and that was a lot better than many of the sons of her friends and cousins, and she wasn't one to tempt fate by complaining.

My father, on the other hand, had made it clear in small ways that he thought Mary was too bossy, too sharp-tongued. "You need a wife who will treat you like an equal," he had said to me several times. "That woman talks to you like you work for her."

"It's a relationship, Dad," I'd said. "Modern women work twice as hard to succeed as men do, and sometimes Mary has a hard time leaving that attitude behind at the office."

He had only snorted. By the time Mary and I divorced, he was already suffering from the cancer that would kill him, and I was locked up in California. Our brief phone calls centered around his health, though I could tell he was happy that Mary had moved on.

Then he had passed away, I inherited his townhouse, and I moved back to my hometown, my tail between my legs.

A lot had happened since then, much of it good, and I hoped that Arielle would have the same ability to rebound from her divorce.

I threw together a quick salad and by the time Lili returned downstairs, dinner was ready. We ate, we talked about our days, and then we retired upstairs to the bedroom, each of us with something to read, with Rochester sprawled at the end of the bed between us.

After a while he stood up and sat on his haunches, staring at us. Lili and I knew the routine; the first one to make eye contact had eighty pounds of golden retriever climbing over him or her. I only held out for a minute; I could feel Rochester's big brown eyes drilling into me with laser intensity.

I put down my Kindle and looked at his dark pupils, surrounded by dark brown iris, with just a hint of white sclera in the background. He moved daintily between Lili and me, and then slumped down, resting most of his body against my chest. I petted him, but he didn't look at me. I got his profile, while his gaze was fixed on Lili.

Eventually she gave up too, closing the book of photographs she was perusing. She put it on the bedside table and turned to the dog. With me scratching his back and her fingers grazing through his chest mane, he was finally happy.

The next morning, I walked Rochester as the sun was rising, making the dew-drenched lawns of River Bend sparkle. It was chilly, requiring my heavy wool jacket, and I wondered if many people would turn out that weekend for the food trucks.

They weren't a new idea—I had often eaten from sandwich trucks when I was in graduate school at Columbia, but back then they weren't gourmet operations, and they depended on foot traffic from the university. Would suburbanites drive into the center of town and wait in the cold for their food? I'd see on Saturday.

I hoped for Arielle's sake things would work out. River Bend was a great place to raise kids, close to downtown and the park along the Delaware River, in a great school district. But property taxes and our association maintenance fees were high. If she couldn't make a success of her food truck, she might have to move somewhere less expensive.

And Rochester would lose his girlfriend.

# Chapter 2
## *Starting Over*

That Friday morning I had a meeting scheduled with John William Babson, Eastern's president. His secretary had sent the meeting request via Outlook, our email program, and there was no indication of what he wanted to discuss. I had accepted, hoping that would generate an agenda—but no.

I had been running the conference center at Friar Lake for two years by then, and I'd had my performance review three months before, with the assistant vice president for facilities. He had commended me for bringing the center into the black in only the second year of operation, and been pleased with the variety of courses I had developed for faculty, alumni and members of the community. I had done a good job as well at renting the facility out to local and national groups, and that had helped the bottom line.

I had every reason to believe President Babson wasn't going to criticize me, but I was still nervous as Rochester and I drove up the River Road to Friar Lake. The swamp maples at the river's edge were barren and hunched, and I glimpsed bits of gray-blue river through the branches.

An order of Catholic monks had built the complex of buildings, then known as Our Lady of the Waters, over a hundred years before, of local gray stone. When I started at the property, I supervised the renovation of the monks' dormitory into high-tech guest rooms, the conversion of the arched-roof chapel into a reception space, and the expansion of several of the outbuildings into classrooms.

My office was in the former gatehouse, and I pulled up in front of it and let Rochester out. As in River Bend, the lawns, tinted a wintry brown, were covered in glistening dew, and Rochester's paws and underbelly were soaked by the time he returned after a quick nose and pee.

I checked my email, hoping for a clue about the meeting with President Babson, but found nothing. There was an announcement from the provost, our chief academic officer, and I clicked through to that.

"The Eastern community was shaken three months ago by the death of Tyler Benjamin, a promising young scholar-athlete midway through his junior year at Eastern," the email read. "Tyler ran track, pursued a major in history, and participated in numerous student groups. Despite his frequent contact with faculty and staff, however, no one noticed the signs of increasing agitation and pressure until it was too late."

I remembered the story. On an evening in mid-November, Tyler's body had been discovered in his dorm room by his roommate. The initial diagnosis had been an opioid overdose, thought to be accidental in nature. But a review of his private journal, and anonymous Internet postings traced to his PC, revealed a young man who was overwhelmed by academic and athletic pressure. He was the first in his family to attend college, on an athletic scholarship.

During the summer he had torn a ligament in his leg and been prescribed pain-killers, and developed an addiction to them as he realized they could blunt his fear of failure. It was unclear what the trigger for his suicide was, but the whole college had been shaken.

Teddy bears, flowers, and track T-shirts were piled near the entrance to his dorm, and his team organized a candlelight procession through campus, which Lili and I had attended. The somber faces of students and faculty moved both of us to tears, even though neither of us knew the young man.

I remembered my own years at Eastern. My father had a degree from a technical school that eventually began to grant college diplomas, and my mother had taken a number of college classes but never received a degree. In a sense my situation was similar to Tyler's, though I wasn't an athlete and certainly never felt as much pressure as it appeared he did.

My four years at Eastern had been an experience that formed my mind, made long-lasting friendships, and gave me the chance to have some fun and grow up. It was sad that current students could react negatively to those opportunities.

The provost ended his message with a promise to institute new programs at Eastern that would help faculty and staff recognize the early warning signs of overwhelming depression and/or opioid abuse, and called upon the entire community to make a commitment to helping those students in need.

Resident assistants in the dorms would be required to attend programs educating them on how to recognize symptoms of depression, suicidal ideations, and drug and alcohol abuse. Faculty would receive similar training focused on the services provided by the college and how to refer students to them. A consultant from the Disney Institute, which emphasized customer service, would work with administrative staff to develop a more user-friendly attitude from the moment a student walked into a campus office.

I thought about the students I had taught as an adjunct in the English Department. Were there signs among them I had missed? Sure, I had some students who showed up to class in a red-eyed stupor—but were they high, or short of sleep? I had students who had missed several assignments in a row. Were they crippled by doubt, or lazy? It was so hard to tell.

At ten o'clock I walked Rochester down to Joey Capodilupo's office. Joey was my counterpart at Friar Lake; he managed the upkeep of all the facilities, from having the lawns mowed and the streets swept of snow to fixing minor plumbing programs. He had a golden retriever of his own, a white bundle of energy named Brody, and whenever I had to head to campus I left Rochester with Joey.

"Did you read that email from the provost?" Joey said, as I walked into his office, cluttered with piles of manuals for every piece of equipment on the property. "I had a teammate when I played baseball for Eastern who got hooked on painkillers after he broke his arm. He ended up switching to marijuana, then eventually to coke. He got desperate for his next hit and killed his dealer. He's doing twenty years in a prison up in coal country now."

"Wow. Did you see the signs of what was going on?"

"My buddy quit the team when he couldn't play and lost his athletic scholarship, so he disappeared. Next I heard of him was what I read in the papers. I know his sister, though, and she says he's doing well now, finishing his college work online."

"At least he had the chance to start over. That poor kid last semester didn't."

I thought more about that as I drove up the few miles inland to Leighville. It was a small town that had boomed in the 19$^{th}$ century when coal moved along the Delaware Canal. The clayey soil of the Delaware Valley was perfect for the manufacture of porcelain and tile. Down the river in Trenton, artists like Walter Scott Lenox were making fancy china to rival the best Europeans, but in Leighville Joseph Fields chose to concentrate on useful items like toilet fixtures and floor tiles. They flowed out of his factories, along the canals that paralleled the shallow Delaware all the way to Philadelphia.

Rather than create a foundation to do charitable works and revere his portrait, Fields left Eastern the bulk of his estate, several million dollars' worth of steel and coal stocks. His mansion, Fields Hall, dominated the hill. Long dormitories flanked the oval drive, fraternities and sororities sat on either side of the gates, and new construction spread over the back side of the hill. Only the main lawn, within the arc of the driveway, remained untouched. It was shaded by ancient elms and provided a pleasant place to relax or study on warm afternoons. A wrought iron fence topped with sunbursts protected it from the clamor of Main Street, which stretched away east to the center of Leighville.

In early March, though, the lawn was deserted as I hurried into Fields Hall. I walked down the narrow hallway, lined with pen and ink drawings of the campus in the 1880s, and into the executive suite.

I greeted Babson's secretary, Cecilia Sanchez, a beautiful Venezuelan in her forties who favored white blouses and scarves in brilliant colors. That morning's looked like it had been taken from one of Monet's lily paintings. She said that President Babson was on the phone, and she'd buzz him as soon as he was free.

"Any idea what he wants to see me for?" I asked.

She shook her head. "But you're not the only one he's calling in. I booked him six of these mystery meetings for today."

I spent a couple of moments thinking of anything I'd been involved with recently that might have involved six people, and in the end I was comforted that this summons wasn't related to something I'd done. I settled down to read a copy of the *Rising Sun*, the student newspaper. Back when I was an undergraduate, it had come out every day, providing students cushioned by Leighville's remoteness with a digest of national events and reports on campus activities.

Since then, every student had a smart phone to get the national news, and the *Rising Sun* had shrunk to six pages once a week. I was in the middle of an editorial on the need for an additional popcorn machine at student events when Cecilia said, "He can see you now."

President Babson had aged since I first returned to Eastern some five years before, but it was hard to tell. His jet-black hair (now expertly dyed, I believed) was slicked down, and he had the vitality of a much younger man. "Steve. Thanks for coming in this morning."

I had heard rumors that he might retire when he reached sixty-five, in a year or so, but I doubted it. He lived and breathed our very good small college, and I couldn't imagine him doing anything other than running it.

He motioned me to the seat across from him, a Windsor-backed chair embossed with the college seal, a sun rising over verdant countryside with the motto 'In Lumine Tuo Recipimus Scientia,' loosely translated as 'In Thy Light We Receive Knowledge.'

"Did you read the email from the provost this morning?"

I nodded. "The suicide was very sad, but I was pleased at the way the college community reacted."

"We're continuing that reaction," he said. "I'm putting together a committee to generate programs to ensure that nothing like this happens again, at least if we can prevent it. I want to use Friar Lake for the delivery of some of these programs, which is why I want you on the committee. Start thinking about what you think you can do."

He sat back in his chair, his hands steepled in front of him. "Sometimes we have to change the environment to generate a different response. I'm thinking we could bring students out to Friar Lake for group discussions about recognizing and reporting at-risk behavior among their friends and classmates, for example."

"I'm pleased to help. I was thinking about Tyler Benjamin this morning, and how we all go through tough times in our lives. You, and Eastern, helped me reboot after my divorce and my time in prison. I'd love to work on some ideas for you, and this committee."

He pushed back his chair and stood up. "Good man. I knew I could count on you, Steve."

I shook his hand and walked out. My old friend Jackie Conrad, a professor in the Department of Natural Sciences, was waiting in the outer office, but we barely had time to say hello before Babson called her in.

I figured she was going to be on this committee as well. The sciences were notorious for the pressure their students were under. The material was difficult and required a lot of memorization, and high grades were essential for pre-med students.

As I drove back to Friar Lake, I reflected on what I had said to Babson. After I graduated from Eastern, I moved to New York, where I got a master's in English from Columbia and met Mary Schulweiss.

I followed her to California, where we married, and she became pregnant with our first child.

She miscarried and went on a retail therapy spree that put us deep into credit card debt. I worked overtime and freelance jobs to dig us out, using the computer skills I developed at my technical writing job. Then she got pregnant again—and miscarried.

I was determined that she couldn't drag us into debt again, so I hacked into the three major credit bureaus and put a flag on her account. Back then, hacking was easier, and I was young and cocky and impressed with my own abilities.

I got caught and served a year as a guest of the California state penal system. During that time Mary divorced me, and my father died and left me the town house in River Bend. When I returned there, one of the first people to believe in me was the chair of the English Department at Eastern, who had been one of my professors.

He gave me a job as an adjunct teaching freshman comp, and that put me in touch with President Babson, who moved me into a full-time job in the alumni relations office. From there I'd moved on to Friar Lake.

I owed Babson, and Eastern College, a great deal. I'd be happy to do what I could to give back to the community, and maybe help someone else in trouble see that there was help available.

When I got back to Friar Lake, Rochester greeted me like he was worried he'd never see me again. I petted his soft head and thought that I'd try and incorporate him into a program at Friar Lake. "Would you do that, boy?" I asked. "Could you be a service dog for troubled students? Help them relax when they're under pressure?"

He looked up at me with a big grin. That was the golden for you. Always willing to provide love and attention.

I began reading about programs to help at-risk college students. Many colleges had instituted drug awareness and suicide prevention programs, including online and face-to-face workshops, guest speakers and a profusion of flyers advertising twenty-four-hour help lines.

I was struck by some of the statistics I read. As in Tyler Benjamin's case, substance abuse and mental disorders account for approximately 90 percent of those who died by suicide. It seemed like the two problems were intertwined.

I made lists of the internal and external factors that might lead to suicide. I was no psychologist or psychiatrist, so I couldn't personally deal with those factors, but I could use them to generate programming ideas. I knew that Eastern put on programs every year on all kinds of topics, but one of the problems organizers ran into was getting students to attend events. Either they didn't want to admit they had problems, or they were too busy to devote the time.

My immediate reaction to that was food. Even though I had the meal plan at Eastern when I was an undergrad, I was always hungry, and I showed up for events when they offered free pizza, popcorn, sodas or desserts. I thought of Arielle and her food truck, and wondered if Eastern could hire her to provide food at some of our events.

That is, if her food was any good. I'd check it out the next day.

I made a note of that as Joey came into my office. Of course Rochester jumped up to greet him, nuzzling his crotch as he sat down. "I keep thinking about that poor kid," Joey said. "Why didn't anyone help him before it got too late?"

"You said that when your friend dropped off the team, you lost touch with him. I'm not saying it was your fault, but that's one of the warning signs. Kids who give up on activities, stop coming to class."

"Doesn't Eastern already have an alert system for that?"

"We do. But in my experience as an adjunct, I know that often problems don't come to a head until it's too late. It's the end of the term before I realize that a student has been absent a few days in a row, or hasn't handed in the last couple of assignments. I know, that's on me to do a better job of keeping track. But if it's the end of the term, and the kid drops out... well, I don't know that anyone follows up."

"My dad used to use this phrase. *In loco parentis*," Joey said. "That we have to look out for these kids as if we were their parents."

His father, Joe Senior, had recently retired as director of facilities for Eastern. "Yeah, I hear that, too. But I believe that we have to work with parents, instead of in place of them." I turned to my computer. "That gives me an idea."

I typed out a couple of sentences about programs for parents that we could run during the times when they were most likely to be on campus: move-in, parents' weekend, graduation and so on. We could invite them out to Friar Lake, away from the hubbub of the campus, and give them a chance to connect with their kids before leaving them to our ministrations.

Joey left a few minutes later, but I kept thinking about ideas as I worked on mundane tasks that afternoon. I took Rochester for a run around the grounds of Friar Lake as the sky began to darken from blue to purple. I noticed for the first time some buds on the oaks and maples. Spring was coming, and with it the promise of new life. It was up to all of us at Eastern to make sure our students understood that we were there to help them face the disappointments of winter along with the promise of spring.

When I got home that evening, I found Lili in the dining room, with those art portfolios spread around the dining room table. I looked over her shoulder at a series of portraits of young women in partial shadow. The photographer had captured the kind of detail I associated with Dutch Renaissance paintings—the way the light glanced off a container of yogurt on the desk behind one girl, for example. "Wow, these are terrific," I said.

"She's incredibly talented," Lili said. "But I'm worried that she's over-taxing herself. She has an Instagram account where she photographs clothes that manufacturers send her. Between that and her classwork she hardly has time for any of this."

"You're smart to keep an eye on her." I told her about my meeting with President Babson that morning, and the effort to create programming for at-risk students. "One of the articles I read focused on the connection between mental illness and creative expression."

She looked up at me. "You're not saying that I'm crazy because I take photos, are you?"

"You're crazy because you love me," I said, kissing her cheek.

"I'm glad that Babson has pulled you into this effort. You care about people, and you like to nose into problems. I think you'll do a great job."

"We all have to. Lives are at stake."

# Chapter 3
## *Food for the Soul*

Saturday morning, Lili continued going through her portfolios while I read the newspaper, then sat with Rochester. The fine hair beside his ears, which reminded me of the *payess* worn by Orthodox Jews, had become tangled, and I got the special comb I'd bought and began to tease the strands clear. I'd read somewhere that petting a dog had physical effects like reducing your heart rate and raising your endorphin levels, and I believed it.

He was a sweet boy, but he shed like a monster, and as I combed out tangles and pulled off wads of loose fur, I accumulated enough golden threads to knit a sweater,

By the time I had a plastic grocery bag full of hair, Rochester rolled onto his back and waved his legs in the air like a dying cockroach. That was his sign that he wanted his belly rubbed.

I complied, as I always did.

Around noon, Lili and I loaded Rochester into the back of my aged BMW and we drove to the center of Stewart's Crossing. The town's history dated to the mid-1700s, when a ferry had been established there running between Pennsylvania and New Jersey, and many of the houses that lined Main Street reflected that heritage. Low-roofed homes of native stone were interspersed with gingerbread Victorians, many of them converted into restaurants and real estate offices.

The shopping center just south of the corner of Main and Ferry Roads was a 1960s addition, and when I was a kid it had boomed, anchored by a State Store – the state-run liquor store in Pennsylvania. We'd gone to the laundromat when my mother's washer broke and we waited for repair. We got take-out pizza there, shopped for greeting cards.

With the development of fancy new plazas in the outer suburbs, with their fieldstone fronts and elegant signage, the little center had suffered. The State Store was still there, but many of the small shop fronts along the big U were empty, either papered over or featuring rental signs. It had been built in a bland architectural style, mostly plate-glass storefronts with signs over the doors.

A chunk of the parking lot had been roped off for the food trucks, and we spotted a renovated Airstream trailer with a custom paint job and the words *Arielle's Cuisine de France* in swirling letters along the side.

As we approached the truck, I smelled the rich scent of bread and butter and my mouth watered. There weren't many cars parked in the lot, and Arielle's truck was at the far end of the line, so no other customers had ended up down there.

Arielle was at the front window, her hair pulled back in a sprightly kerchief. "Steve! Thanks for coming by."

I introduced Lili, who said, "It must take a lot of work to get this truck going every day. Too bad you're so far down here away from the customers."

Arielle pushed back a stray hair from her forehead. "It's a free-form thing. Whoever gets here first gets the best spot. I've been up since five, baking and loading the truck, but Brandon was being a pain in the ass getting ready to go into Philly for the day, and so I was late getting out of the house."

She shook her head. "Now that's he's officially a teen-ager, I worry so much about him getting into drugs that I watch every single thing. Every time he wants to stay in his room instead of playing a board game with Sophia and me, or says he wants to go out with some friend I've never heard of, I worry. I've read so much about teens and drugs that I'm on overload."

"And doesn't Pierre help?" I asked.

"He wants to be the fun dad so much that I think he ignores these warning signs, and lets Brandon get away with too much. Last week he had the kids for the weekend, and when I called on Saturday night to say good night Pierre said Brandon had gone to a party. He didn't know the kid's name, or where the party was. He kept saying that Brandon knew he had a curfew, and he would be home. I told him that's not good enough for a thirteen-year-old."

"I don't know much about raising kids, but I'd agree with that," Lili said. "My friends who have teens always want to know where the kids will be and whose parents are going to be supervising."

Arielle leaned against the side of the window, and I wondered how she'd manage to both cook and serve if things got busy. "I'd like to get the kids into counseling because of the divorce, but I can't afford it and Pierre doesn't think it's necessary. He has decided he's 'finding himself' as the head of a non-profit, but he's not making anywhere near the income he could if he went back into corporate law."

I looked at Lili. We made do on our college salaries, but I could see that if we had the expense of raising a pair of kids we'd need more money.

"Pierre gives me alimony and child support, but that doesn't begin to cover all the expenses that go with raising a pair of twenty-first century kids like martial arts and ballet and Hebrew school and all their devices and memberships."

She sighed. "Sometimes I think I ought to chuck it all in and get a job that would let me spend more time with the kids, but there isn't anything else I can do." She wiped a tear from her eyes.

I didn't want Arielle getting weepier, so I tried to change the subject. "Are these all the trucks?"

"The only one of our usual crew who's missing is Roly, *El Rey de los Pollos*, the king of the chickens." Arielle laughed. "Roly was late for his own wedding, the birth of each of his four kids, and he'll be late for his own funeral."

"Tell me about it," Lili said. "I'm Cuban and I'm the only one in my family who doesn't run at least fifteen minutes late for everything."

"If you're Cuban, then when Roly gets here you have to try his food. His dad owns a chain of restaurants in North Jersey."

I looked around at the trucks. "Interesting variety."

"There are two kinds of food trucks, what we call the natives and the hipsters," Arielle said. "I'm a hipster, because I'm young, I'm a trained chef, and I like to experiment with food."

She pointed to her display. "I like to fiddle with different fillings for my croissants. Today's special is mushroom and kale, though so far I haven't had any takers."

We opted to go traditional, and ordered a couple of rich, fragrant chocolate croissants, baked fresh that morning, and cups of café au lait. As I was paying, the guy at the next truck, Otto's Organic, put out a tall outdoor heater to keep his customers warm in the spring chill. He was in his late twenties, with a bodybuilder's bulk and tattoos snaking out along his arms from under his short-sleeved shirt.

"Hey, Arielle," he called.

She answered him, then turned to us. "That's Otto. He's another hipster, a cooking school grad who worked as a private chef until he got together the cash to set up his own truck." She pointed down the row. "Mariana and Carmela are a couple whose specialty is gourmet burgers, and Michael, down the way, ran his own restaurant into the ground and reinvented himself as a sandwich king."

Her cell phone rang, and we stood there, nibbling our croissants and drinking our coffee, as she spoke. "Oh, no, you can't do this to me, Keenwa. Especially not on such short notice. Saturday is always our best day and I need the help."

# *Dog Willing*

I looked around, and indeed, the parking lot was filling up and singles, couples and families were drifting our way.

Arielle listened for a moment, then finally ended the call. "That was my assistant, Keenwa. She handles the register while I cook and package up the food, and she can't make it today. She says she's sick, but I think she probably just wants to play hooky. My two best friends took a bunch of kids, including Brandon and Sophia, on a field trip to the Franklin Institute Science Museum, so I can't ask either of them."

She looked ready to cry again. "I should just shut down and go home."

"I can help you," I said. "I worked a register for a while when I was in high school. It comes back to you, doesn't it? Like riding a bike?"

"That would be awesome, Steve. Thank you so much!"

Lili took Rochester's leash. "I've been wanting to take some pictures of Rochester in that park down by the Delaware. Suppose we come back for you in two hours or so?"

"That's perfect," Arielle said. "That'll get me through the lunch rush. If that's okay with you, Steve?"

"Just show me what to do."

Lili left a few minutes later and I joined Arielle inside the trailer. "What kind of a name is Keenwa?"

"She's named after the grain, quinoa. Her mother liked the sound of it but she didn't know how to spell it, so she did it phonetically." She laughed. "Otto's always telling her that with a name like hers she ought to work at his truck instead of mine."

She walked me over to the register and showed me how it worked. She had a gadget that accepted credit cards, and I learned what I had to type in and how to swipe the cards. Then the lunch rush began. Arielle made sandwiches and crepes, and I served up the pre-packaged baked goods and sodas and coffee and took payments.

In between customers, we chatted. "Can I ask you a question, Steve? It's sort of personal."

"You can ask."

"I know you've been divorced, and I wonder if men feel the same way women do after a divorce. Like, I loved Pierre, even though he had his faults. But now that we've split up I keep going back and wondering how I overlooked so many of those warning signs."

"For example?"

"He's always been very pompous and full of himself. I assumed that was because he was an attorney. A lot of the men he worked with were the same way. But should his lousy behavior have set off warning bells a long time ago?" She paused and licked her lips. "My cousin said something once, that he was too handsome for his own good. And maybe I was just being shallow."

"It's pretty common that once the love wears away you focus on the bad stuff," I said. "I was thinking about my ex the other day, and how my parents never really liked her but wouldn't come out and say anything. They were able to see the faults that I ignored. And now, even years later, it's hard to remember anything other than the bad things."

I looked over at Arielle, who was staring intently. "How is Pierre with your kids?"

"Pierre was always the fun dad. He let the kids get away with everything, and his favorite thing was to sit with them at night and read them French nursery rhymes and stories. He'd never discipline them directly, just complain to me. We used to take the kids to Styer's apple orchard. You know it?"

"Sure."

"I always worried about them hurting their teeth on those candy apples, and when they asked me I'd say no, but then a few minutes later I'd see them each chewing away with Pierre. It used to make me crazy."

"Uh-oh," I said. "I did the same thing with my dad. My mom would say no to a candy apple, and then I'd ask him and he'd say yes. I never thought about it from my mom's perspective."

"Other than the nursery rhymes, Pierre was pretty hands-off with the kids until a couple of years ago when Brandon had a serious bout with Lyme disease. That really turned Pierre around. He became this obsessive helicopter parent and fought with me all the time about what I was letting the kids do, who they played with, what activities they joined."

She took a sip of her coffee. "Then he decided he wanted to get out of law and shift his career into something non-profit. I didn't like that idea and I was not supportive at all."

"Why not? Why wouldn't you be happy Pierre wants to do something good with his life?"

"I don't believe him. He didn't shift jobs until we were determined to divorce, and I think it was a way to screw me out of alimony. And in the end it's all a front to get custody of the kids. Like he can portray himself as a saint, while I care more for my business than Brandon and Sophia."

A couple of customers came to the window and we got busy again, but while I waited for people to dig out their cash or credit cards, I thought about what Arielle had said. I had never met Pierre, so it was hard to make a judgment based solely on Arielle's portrait, but something didn't seem right.

The next time we had a lull, Arielle pointed out more of the trucks. The "natives," as she called them, were a mixed bunch, serving up Haitian, Jamaican and Peruvian cuisine, working from old family recipes, as well as an Italian family making pizza and stromboli. Roly had pulled in on the other side of her, at the very end of the line of trucks, but he had no shortage of customers, especially once the smell of his roasted chickens filled the air.

Each truck brought a few tables and chairs which had been set up in a communal area. Roly had a killer sound system, and he serenaded customers with a combination of sixties hits and Cuban folk music. The vibe was happy and friendly—until an angry woman in a beige pants suit and heavy brown shoes stomped over.

"Oh, crap, that's Darlene Nowak," Arielle said to me. "She runs a little bookstore here in the center, and she hates it when the food trucks take up space in the parking lot."

The woman she called Darlene stopped in front of Otto's truck. "You're blocking the entrance to my store," she said, in a grating, nasally voice.

"No, we're not, Darlene," Otto said. "There's plenty of room for your customers to get into the lot and park in front of your store."

"But they can't even see me with your horrendous trucks blocking the view."

I looked across from us to where her store, Book Crossing, was sandwiched between an empty storefront and a karate dojo. Her windows need cleaning, and the shelves behind them were haphazardly stacked with a mix of hardcover and paperback books.

"They can see your sign out by the street," Otto said. "And who knows, maybe some of our customers will need something to read."

Darlene sneered. "Your customers don't read. And they clearly don't have taste, or they wouldn't be buying from you."

"She's a charmer, isn't she?" Arielle whispered to me. "What a god-awful person."

The dark-haired Latina Arielle had called Mariana leaned out the service window of her truck. "Go back into your store, book bitch," she called, in a heavy accent. "You stay out here much longer you'll scare away the customers!"

"I'm calling the police and the health department!" Darlene screeched.

"We've got our permits, and every one of our trucks has passed the health inspection," Otto said. "If you'd taste our food, you'd see we're doing a service for this shopping center."

"What kind of a service takes away my business?" she asked.

"She has a tiny café in the back of her store, where she pours ordinary coffee and serves warehouse store pastries, usually stale," Arielle said to me. "There is no way the gourmet high-quality food we serve is taking any business from her."

"Come on, Darlene. Let me put together a selection of food from our trucks for you. Call it food for the soul."

I looked out the window. I could see the emotions warring on Darlene's face. She hated these trucks. But free food? Like the kids at Eastern College, I doubted she'd pass up the offer.

Though I wouldn't be surprised if she took it all and resold it in her own café.

"Fine. But you'd better make it good." She turned and stalked back into her store.

A few minutes later, Otto put out a big platter on a table in front of his truck with a handmade sign that read "Food for Darlene." Reluctantly, Arielle pulled out two pre-made *croque monsieur* sandwiches, one flaky croissant filled with baked ham and melted cheese, the other her kale special—which was not selling at all. She carried them over to the table and put them down.

We got a couple of customers, and the next time I looked at the table in front of Otto's there was a pile of food on the platter. I went back to work and didn't notice who took the platter over to the bookstore.

Arielle and I worked steadily through the lunch rush, and it was fun to be doing something so different from what I normally did. But by the time the rush was over, I was tired, my feet hurt, and my back felt cramped. "How do you manage this all day?" I asked, as I washed my hands.

"You get used to it. This is an easy gig, because it's a lunch crowd, and it's all daylight. When we do a night event, like we're doing in Levittown Monday evening, we get bigger crowds and we work a lot harder. Some of the venues are great, with lots of trees and tables and chairs, but a couple are in bad neighborhoods, or right near places where rats and lizards and possums gather. Sometimes we have to put out rat poison to keep the animals away."

She wanted to pay me for my help, but I refused. "Thank you so much, Steve. It would have been a real madhouse here without your help, and I would have lost a lot of sales from people who didn't want to wait."

"I'm going to walk over to the bookstore. I didn't even know we had one in town."

"Don't be offended if Darlene is nasty to you. That's the way she is." She shook her head. "Honestly, I don't know how her store survives. She's not a welcoming salesperson."

I walked toward the store, and as I got closer, I saw that the haphazard display of books I'd noticed before focused on mysteries, all of them by women authors. Was it a special promotion? There was nothing to indicate that, nor did it seem like it was a feminist or lesbian bookstore.

I pushed open the door and the bell tinkled, but no one came out to help me. I browsed around for a while, and finally picked out a book to buy, a cute paperback in what was called the Dead-End Job series by an author named Elaine Viets. "Hello?" I called. "Anyone here?"

No answer. I walked to the back of the store, where a door was open to a small office behind with the back window open and a chill breeze blowing through. And there I found Darlene Nowak, slumped at her desk, a half-eaten croque monsieur in front of her and a pile of vomit beside it. There was a slight white crust around her mouth—probably dried puke. The smell was awful, but I couldn't just leave her there.

I edged closer, looking for signs that she was breathing but not seeing any. "Hello? Are you okay?"

When I got no answer, I reached for her neck, to take her pulse, but her skin was cold to the touch.

At least this was a death no one could blame on Rochester. My detective dog was still out being photographed by Lili.

# Chapter 4
## *Not Our Monkeys*

I didn't touch anything, and I used my own cell phone to call 911. Then I called my friend Rick Stemper, a detective on the Stewart's Crossing police force. As soon as he answered, he said, "I've got another call from dispatch. Let me call you back later."

He hung up without giving me a chance to explain. That's fine; all I wanted was him to know about the death and that I was there. He'd see me soon enough.

I went back outside to tell Arielle what I'd discovered. "One of my dishes! How could that be?"

"It looked like she had a heart attack. Nothing to do with your food. You saw how angry she was. Probably spiked her blood pressure."

It had gotten chilly as the sun hid behind clouds, and I moved my chair closer to the warming tower Otto had set up. I realized that I had walked out of the store with the book, but I wasn't going back in there to return it. I put the book on one of the tables and sat with Arielle, who was still upset as a police car turned into the shopping center, red and blue lights flashing, and moved slowly through the lot as the crowds parted to let it through.

Only a minute behind was Rick's truck. Instead of following the black and white, he pulled into the first available spot and headed toward us. Rick was my age; we'd known each other back in high school, but we hadn't become friends until I returned to Stewart's Crossing and we bonded over our bitter divorces.

Our forties were treating him better—he was slimmer than I was, though his short-cropped dark hair showed a few more streaks of gray than mine did. He held up his hand as he approached, palm up. "Don't even tell me," he said. "Or, don't tell me until I see what's going on."

He looked around. "Where's the death dog?"

That was his less than flattering nickname for Rochester, who had a disturbing tendency of discovering dead bodies. "This one's all on me. Rochester's off with Lili."

He blew out a deep breath and followed the first uniformed officer into the bookstore, while the second remained by the front door to keep the curious at bay.

A couple of minutes later two more black-and-whites showed up, along with an officer on a Segway who swerved around through the crowd. They blocked off the entrance to the lot and wouldn't let anyone leave without giving their name and contact information.

After about ten minutes, a cop came by and told us that all of the food truck personnel would have to remain for interviews. "It's ridiculous," Otto grumbled as we waited. "I have another rally tonight and I need to get back home and do some prep work. And Ramon needs to head out to his other job."

"Ramon is Otto's helper," Arielle said to me, when Otto walked away. "See that good-looking guy over there?"

"Not very helpful," I said.

"The tall one with the dark hair and the soul patch," Arielle said. "I think he looks like a movie star."

"Probably a model in his spare time."

"Not Ramon. I feel so bad for him. He went to one of those rip-off for-profit colleges to get his certificate as a medical assistant. But before he could finish, the school closed, and he can't get anywhere to accept his transfer credits. And on top of that somebody crashed into his car on I-95 and he got hurt pretty badly. It's taken him a long time to bounce back."

"Poor guy. I've had a couple of students in the past who've had that kind of one-two punch that knocks them out, so I know how tough it is to come back." I didn't mention that I'd had my own troubles in that regard.

Lili arrived with Rochester a few minutes later. I told her what had happened, and she shook her head. "I leave you alone for an hour, and you find a body. You're turning Stewart's Crossing into Cabot Cove."

I didn't appreciate the remark comparing me to Jessica Fletcher, the fictional sleuth who lived in a small town in Maine. "I think there are a few differences between me and Angela Lansbury," I said. Lansbury was the actress who'd starred in a dozen seasons of the fictional drama. "For one, my hair is not as gray."

"Keep finding bodies, it'll get there."

Rochester was not content to stand there, so while Lili walked over to Arielle I took him for a walk. He was wild to sniff everything in the area, all the dropped bits of food and crumpled wrappers, and I had to grab his leash and walk him around for a bit. He stopped every two feet to sniff something, and I had to keep tugging him along. "No, you can't eat that. If you aren't going to pee on that, move along."

We walked behind the food trucks, where the owners had left out big plastic tubs and garbage cans, and Rochester stopped to sniff a sandwich bag. "Oh, no, you don't need whatever is inside that," I said, pulling on his leash. He didn't want to give it up, though, so I looked down at it.

There was a fine bluish-white powder inside the bottom, and I wondered what it was. It resembled the crust I'd seen around Darlene Nowak's mouth. It could have been anything—a kid's vitamin crushed under his sandwich, a bit of sea salt—but I had learned to trust Rochester's instincts.

I pulled a tissue from my pocket and picked it up by the corner where the zipper ended, careful not to let anything fall out. Then I struggled to direct Rochester back to the table where Lili waited, though he wanted to keep exploring.

Lili, Arielle and I watched as Rick and Jerry Vickers, the other detective in the department, moved from truck to truck, talking to the vendors. I realized that it was the first time I'd seen Rick and Jerry work at the same crime scene, probably because there were so many people to talk with at the food truck rally.

As soon as either of them was finished with a truck, the vendor shut down and drove away, until Arielle was one of the last few left. Jerry Vickers took Arielle into the kitchen to talk about the food, while Rick joined me, Lili and Rochester at the plastic table. He kissed Lili's cheek, petted Rochester, and sat down across from me. "Walk me through how you found yet another dead body," Rick said. "I'm not keeping count, but if I didn't know you I'd be very suspicious."

I'd had time to think while I waited for him. Caroline Kelly, Rochester's first owner, in a wooded area near the entrance to River Bend. Joe MacCormac, a mentor of mine at Eastern, in a snowbank outside Fields Hall. A half-decayed body buried on the grounds of Friar Lake, and the skeletal remains of a 1960s draft-dodger behind a wall at the Friends Meeting House in Stewart's Crossing. An unpleasant dog trainer, a couple of senior citizens at a nursing home in town. My college friend floating face down in the Delaware Canal, and my rabbi's brother on the grounds of the synagogue.

Yeah, it was a long list.

"I've known Arielle casually for a couple of years, because our dogs play together," I began. "The other day she told me about this food truck rally and Lili and I came over to see what it's like." I walked him through the call from Keenwa and Arielle's need for a helper.

"You volunteered? Though you hardly know her?"

"She's going through a bad divorce and she didn't have anyone else to call," I said. "It's not like she asked me to help her out with a surgical intervention. I took orders and ran the cash register."

"And then?"

"After we'd been there for about an hour, this woman came up to the trucks and started complaining. They were blocking access to her business, their customers were losers, that kind of thing."

"How did the vendors react?"

"One of the women at the burger truck called her a bitch, but Otto over there was nice to her." Otto had already closed the front window of his truck. He was folding the last of his chairs and sliding them into the side door. "He said that if she tasted the food, she'd come around."

"He's the one who initiated the delivery of food to Mrs. Nowak?"

"That's what I saw." I explained how Arielle had delivered her food to the tray, and how the food piled up quickly after that. "Could anyone have had access to that tray while it was in front of Otto's Organics?" Rick asked.

"Yeah, I guess so. I didn't see who took the tray into the bookstore, so I can't say how long it sat there."

"Okay, good. What next?"

"When things slowed down I went for a walk while I was waiting for Lili and Rochester to come back. I didn't even know that bookstore was there until Mrs. Nowak came out and complained, so I thought I'd check it out."

A couple of crows circled around and landed a few feet from us, pecking at leftover crumbs. "Go slowly. Tell me exactly what you did."

"I walked in and the bell over the door jingled, but no one came out to greet me. I walked around and looked at the books. There was a good selection of paperback mysteries, so I picked one up, read the back cover and decided to buy it." I held up the book. "This one here."

Rick usually took his notes on a small pad he kept in his pocket, but this time he'd brought a small laptop with him, and he typed as I spoke.

"I wanted to pay for the book, so I called out, but no one answered." My heart rate increased as I remembered the scene. "I saw a half-open door to a back area, and I went over there."

"Did you touch the door?"

"I think so. I pushed it open a bit more and called out again. Nobody answered, but then I saw Mrs. Nowak slumped over her desk. She didn't respond when I asked if she was all right. It was cold in there with the window open, and I shivered and rubbed my shoulders. I hesitated for a minute and then I touched her skin lightly with the back of my hand. Her flesh was cold so I stepped out and called 911."

Rick nodded. "You never met Mrs. Nowak before?"

I shook my head. "Like I said, I didn't even realize that bookstore was there, and I've been back in town for ages. I don't see how she made a living there."

I remembered the plastic sandwich bag Rochester had found and used the edge of the book to push it toward him across the table. "It may be nothing, but Rochester sniffed this baggie out behind the trucks a little while ago."

He pulled a pair of blue plastic gloves from the shoulder bag that carried his laptop and slipped them on, then picked up the bag and pulled open the zipper. He leaned in and sniffed. "No discernible odor."

My eyes opened wide. "Isn't it dangerous to inhale that stuff?"

"Don't worry. I've read dozens of reports on how to handle suspicious substances. The chances of this being something deadly just to take a breath of are very, very low. If it was that deadly, we'd see more bodies around here than just Mrs. Nowak."

"Do you recognize the stuff?"

He shook his head. "Could be anything, though it sure doesn't look like the remains of somebody's lunch—which you'd expect it to smell. Knowing Rochester's talents I'll take it in and have it analyzed." He looked at me. "I knew the death dog was going to get involved in this at some point."

He got an evidence bag from his laptop case and wrote the date, time and location on it. Then he slipped the plastic bag inside.

Jerry Vickers came out of the truck then. He was about ten years older than Rick and I were, with thinning hair and a pot belly.

Rick folded his laptop. "I'll get back to you later," he said, and he walked up to Vickers. They talked as they walked away.

Arielle came outside then. "Everything okay?" I asked her.

"I told him that I prepared the *croque monsieurs* myself. There couldn't be anything wrong with them. But he kept insisting that there was a possibility that the food had been poisoned. He wanted to know about every argument we'd had with Darlene. It was boring and repetitive."

She looked at her watch. "*Merde!* I didn't realize it was so late. My kids will be home from Philadelphia soon."

I picked up my book and hooked Rochester's leash and Lili, Rochester and I walked back through the parking lot toward the street. The only other truck remaining was Roly's, and Rick and Jerry were talking to him. It seemed like he was very agitated by their questions. Rochester strained to go over there but I reined him in. "Not our circus, not our monkeys," I said to him. It was an expression I'd heard recently, that was a lot more colorful than "we need to mind our own business."

# Chapter 5
## *Dinner Date*

That night, Lili and I had a dinner date with Joey Capodilupo and his partner, Mark Figueroa. I had known Mark, an antique dealer in Stewart's Crossing, since I moved to town, and I'd been the one to fix him up with Joey. Seeing them together always reminded me that I had a vested interest in their continuing happiness.

What would happen if they broke up, though? I'd still have to work with Joey, so would I take his side in arguments? Would I lose my friendship with Mark?

I pushed those thoughts aside. The guys seemed very happy together, and there was no reason to worry about something with no basis in reality.

The guys arrived at our house at six on Saturday with Brody, their lively white golden retriever. No longer a puppy, he was big enough that when he put his front paws up on my waist he could almost nuzzle my face if I leaned down.

He and Rochester loved each other, and their best times were when Joey brought Brody to work at Friar Lake and the two of them could race around the grounds like gazelles on the plains of Africa.

As soon as I opened the door, Brody rushed in and tackled

Rochester, and the two of them went rolling across the tile floor toward the dining room. "Hey! Don't break anything!" I called.

"How's Brody doing?" Lili asked Joey, after we'd all said hello, kissed and shook hands. Joey was dressed as he often was at Friar Lake, in blue jeans, boots and a white fisherman's sweater. "Steve said you were worried he was losing weight."

"The vet said overactive thyroid, and prescribed him some pills. He's been doing much better, gained back the weight he lost."

"He certainly looks healthy," I said, as I watched him and Rochester tumble around.

Even though I was about six feet tall, both Mark and Joey towered over me, probably the results of good genes and childhood nutrition—Joey at six-four, Mark a reedy six-six. As a matter of fact, one of the reasons I'd fixed them up was that they were both so tall.

Mark wore a new-looking leather jacket over a plaid shirt and jeans. He wanted to try a restaurant in Levittown that had been recommended to him by one of his customers, the Brown Dog Café. Anything dog-related worked for me, so I was happy to agree, and Lili checked the website and found they served American comfort food with contemporary twists, which seemed to please her.

We piled into the big SUV Mark used to move artwork and small pieces of furniture for his store, and he drove us up through the farm-land-turned-suburbs that were between Stewart's Crossing and Levittown.

When I was growing up, Levittown was populated by workers at the Fairless Works, US Steel's open pit mill. With the mill's closure, the area had slid downhill, but now the presence of low-cost housing and an easy commute by highway or train into Philadelphia had drawn a new generation of suburbanites.

The Brown Dog Café was in a strip shopping center anchored by a Pathmark grocery at one end and a huge two-story gym at the other. There were photos of the namesake dog, a Labrador mix, in the front window. "How cute!" Mark said at a photo of the dog on his back, waiting for a belly rub.

We felt right at home, surrounded by doggie knickknacks – embossed bowls, photo frames surrounded by dog bones, and so on. We sat at a four-top near the front window and perused the menu.

I understood the menu theme then. You could get a traditional burger, or you could get it with portobello mushroom or a smoked garlic aioli. The pizza could come with house-smoked toy box tomatoes or farm-raised pork belly. It was pretentious that so many of the ingredients were sourced—did I need to know that the lettuce was from Ohio, for example?

We ordered a platter of house-smoked chicken wings to start, and then a selection of entrées we could share. Then Mark turned to Joey. "Did you remember to give Brody his pill before we left the house?"

"Yes, I did, sweetheart," Joey said, with a long-suffering tone to his voice. He turned to us. "The vet told me the weirdest thing. He has to keep close track of any opioid pills he prescribes for dogs, because apparently some people come in complaining that their dog is in pain. They get the pills and then take them themselves."

"That's awful," I said. "Are they really the same pills?"

"I think so, but they've got to be dosed lower than for humans if they're based on body weight."

"That won't matter for an addict," Mark said. "Trust me, I've run across a few in my life. My aunt and uncle finally had to push away my cousin because he was bleeding them dry. They were paying for his car and his phone and his health insurance, but any money he made went right to pills. They sent him to rehab twice, digging into their retirement money, before they gave up."

"Do you think this suicide stuff we've been getting at Eastern is tied to drug abuse?" Joey asked Lili and me.

We talked about the initiative I had been asked to join, and then dug into our chicken wings. Our conversation segued from drugs and dogs to the food truck event we'd attended that afternoon.

"I go over there sometimes at lunch," Mark said. "I think they'll get better crowds when the weather warms up, though."

"Did you ever go to that bookstore there, Book Crossing?" I asked.

"Most of the books in the window were by women and I wondered if it was a lesbian or gay store."

"I went in once, maybe a year ago," Mark said. "Right after the place opened. You're right, most of the books I saw were by women. And the clerk was kind of rude when I asked for a book I'd heard about. She looked at me like I was some kind of Philistine because I was interested in a best-seller."

"Imagine what she'd think of me," Joey said with a laugh. "I'd be like, 'I'm looking for the latest sports biography.'"

"Well, you don't have to worry about that now," I said. "She's dead."

Conversation stopped for a moment as the server delivered our entrées. "How do you know?" Mark asked.

I explained about how I'd been helping Arielle at her French truck, and then discovered Darlene Nowak's body.

"Don't tell Gail you're helping at that truck," Mark said. "She's really worried that the food trucks in general, and the French pastry truck in particular, are damaging her business."

Our mutual friend Gail Dukowski ran a small café in downtown Stewart's Crossing called The Chocolate Ear, and in addition to a line of custom chocolates, she sold pastries and sandwiches, often with a French flair similar to Arielle's. Though I had yet to see kale on her menu.

"I didn't even think of that," I admitted. "Even though we both ordered chocolate croissants."

"I wouldn't worry about it," Mark said. "Word I have from the town council is that they're going to suspend the permits for those food trucks. They bring too much traffic to the shopping center, tying up the parking spaces so people can't get into the stores."

"But half the stores are empty," I protested.

"Isn't that the point?" Lili asked. "Would you sign a lease in a shopping center where customers would have trouble parking?"

I gave up. I thought any traffic to the center would be better than none, but I did understand that if you needed to make a quick pit stop for something, you wouldn't pull in somewhere where the parking was difficult. And that could lead to different habits.

I had brought home some leftover desserts from Arielle's food truck, so we got the check and drove back to the townhouse, where the dogs welcomed us as if we'd been gone for days instead of a couple of hours. I left Lili and Mark to put out the desserts and brew some cappuccinos, and Joey and I took Rochester and Brody out for a quick walk.

"How's the new house working out?" I asked. In the fall, Mark and Joey had closed on a single-family house in River Bend, far enough from us that it wasn't an easy walk. He and I worked different schedules, so we didn't commute to Friar Lake together except in odd situations, and it was funny to me that once they'd moved from the apartment over Mark's antique store we never talked about the fact that we lived so close.

"I'm almost finished with the work I wanted to do. I got through all the repairs first. Then we painted the whole house. Or should I say I painted, and Mark handed me stuff." He shook his head. "For a guy who can refinish furniture beautifully, he's a klutz when it comes to bigger jobs."

We stopped so that the dogs could sniff and pee. "I put up the new window treatments last weekend. Now I just have to finish some shelves in the storage closet and above the washer and dryer."

We hung out together for a while after that, enjoying the desserts, and then Mark, Joey and Brody went home.

I was puttering around the kitchen when I heard something fall in the living room. I jumped up to find Rochester pawing at the mystery novel I'd picked up at the bookstore. The noise I heard had been him knocking it off the coffee table.

I felt mildly guilty for not paying for the book, and I guess that motivated me to pull out my laptop for some quick research on Book Crossing and Darlene Nowak. The website for the store was so old it could have had cobwebs on it, with nothing more than just the name of the store and directions. It wasn't even a direct URL, just a site underneath a free provider of sites.

It irked me that she hadn't done anything to use that digital real estate. These days, any company has to have a website, even if only to provide hours and directions. But Nowak could have done so much more. She could have listed the kind of books sold in the store, for example. There had to be a place in the market for someone who specialized in female authors, but without something online to tell me, I'd never have known.

She could have listed her best-sellers, or any special events she sponsored like author readings. Arielle had told me the store had a small café—Nowak could have been advertising that, too, though that would have put her in direct competition to Gail Dukowski's Chocolate Ear.

I found an equally dusty LinkedIn profile, one that hadn't been updated at least since Nowak bought the bookstore, which listed her under Darlene Giordano Nowak. I was surprised to discover that she had a BA in creative writing from City College in New York. If she had gone direct from high school to college, she had been fifty-five at the time of her death.

At CCNY she had studied with a writer whose name I recognized, Jamie Quattrone. He was a minor literary figure and along with Norman Mailer, Tom Wolfe and Joan Didion, he was one of the founders of the New Journalism, which adapted fictional techniques to non-fiction.

I couldn't remember the name of the book I'd read by him, so I popped over to Google. The first thing that came up wasn't about his books, though; he had recently purchased an apartment at the Clock Tower Condominium, a historic landmark on the Brooklyn waterfront. The Realtor who represented him was Sherri Svenson, the wife of my grad school friend Tor.

Well, that was an interesting coincidence, I thought as I sat back in my chair. I had two connections to Darlene Nowak: I had found her body, and I knew Sherri, who knew Jamie Quattrone, who had known Darlene as a young woman.

It seemed like a thread I had to follow.

It was only ten o'clock, and I was pretty sure that Tor would still be awake—he lived in Manhattan, the city that never sleeps, right? So I called him.

"Steve! What a nice surprise. But then, you're the kind of guy who always remembers birthdays and anniversaries."

I gulped, and racked my brain. Tor was a Virgo, like me—we had often joked when we lived together about who could be the most compulsively organized. That meant... was it his anniversary?

Tor had met Sherri soon after he graduated from business school, when he and I were sharing an apartment in a rundown building on the Lower East Side. I had my MA in English by then, too, and I was cobbling together a bunch of adjunct teaching jobs with a night proofing job at a law firm.

He and Sherri met at one of those all-Ivy happy hours they used to have in the city—and perhaps still did. I remembered riding the subway home from midtown with him after that party, at the Harvard Club or the Yale Club or one of those, and him crowing that he had met the woman he wanted to marry.

Sure enough, they had dated for a year, then married, six months before the visa that allowed him to work for two years after graduation was about to expire. "Happy anniversary," I said. "The Carlyle Hotel, wasn't it?"

"Ah, you have the best memory of anyone!" He had been in the United States for over thirty years, but he still had a vestige of his Swedish accent, only heard on the occasional word like "have" turned into "half."

"Well, I was your best man," I admitted. "Something like that tends to stick with you."

The memories did indeed come back. Sherri, already a successful real estate agent, had found a deal on a great condo a few blocks east of the Flatiron Building in midtown, and they were planning to move there after the honeymoon. I didn't know where I was going to live until Mary, who I had been dating for about the same length of time as Tor and Sherri, got a job offer in Silicon Valley and asked me to move with her.

And so began a long unhappy saga that I had been trying to put behind me for years.

"How are you, Steve? Still at the college?"

We traded information for a few minutes. Eventually I said, "I was wondering if I could talk to Sherri for a minute. I found her name in something I was searching for online."

"Only something good, I hope."

"A deal she made. For an old-time writer named Jamie Quattrone."

He laughed. "She'll have a lot to tell you about him. He's a talker." He turned away from the phone and called Sherri, and a minute later she was there.

"Hi, Steve. Tor said you wanted to talk about Jamie Quattrone? Have you been reading his books?"

"No, not for ages. But a woman who was one of his students years ago died recently here in Stewart's Crossing, and I was trying to find out a bit more about her. His name came up, and then yours."

"He loves to talk about the old days," she said. "Carousing with Norman Mailer. You know he was at the party where Mailer stabbed his wife."

"Wow. I don't remember ever learning about that in literature classes."

"Well, you were at Columbia. If you'd been at City College I'm sure you would have heard. Did you want to talk to him? Because I'm sure he'd love the chance to tell his old stories again."

I couldn't turn down the chance to talk to a literary idol—or someone who could provide some background on Darlene Nowak, even if it was a few decades old.

She gave me Quattrone's email address, and after more congratulations about the anniversary, and hearing about her kids as teenagers, I hung up.

I went back to my laptop and dashed off an email to Quattrone. I wasn't sure he'd respond, but I told him that I had met a former student of his who had spoken highly of him, and I thought he might want to know that she had passed away. I was eager to hear if he had any memories of her, I wrote, and I'd be happy to come up to Brooklyn to chat, if he was available.

Rochester was curled around my feet at that point, so I didn't have to get up and take him out, and I dug a little deeper online into Darlene Nowak.

First, I went back to that old LinkedIn profile. A year after graduating from City College, she had been accepted into the prestigious Iowa Writer's Workshop, which boasted graduates including Flannery O'Connor and other names that graced the best-seller lists. She must have been quite talented—I knew a grad school friend from Columbia, who I thought was a great writer back then, who hadn't been admitted.

While at Iowa, and in the years after, she had published several short stories in prestigious literary magazines. Sometime after she graduated, she had gotten a grant to teach creative writing on a native American reservation in South Dakota. What in the world had driven a city girl there?

Whatever it was, she'd left after a year and moved to Silicon Valley, just as the dot-com bubble began to grow. After that, her resume was a hodgepodge of short-term jobs in high-tech companies. The last job in her background was with a company I recognized.

Bestnames.com was founded by a couple of guys who spent a fortune buying up every conceivable internet domain and then reselling them to people who wanted to start businesses. For a while they owned sites like besttoiletpaper.com and howtowinatpoker.com. They built up a business buying and selling these names, then launched an initial public offering right around the time Mary got pregnant with our first child.

I was too busy with my job and my life to pay much attention, but the IPO soared. Then after the initial 90-day lockdown period ended, insiders began selling their shares and the value of the business tanked. It was one of the first high-profile firms to fail.

If Darlene Nowak had worked there, especially if she'd lost money in the crash, no wonder she was bitter.

That was all LinkedIn had to tell me, so I went back to my search engine. I discovered that Stewart's Crossing Center LLC was suing Nowak for back rent and trying to evict her. According to public records, Nowak, who was the sole owner of the store, had not paid any rent for the last six months. I also found a lien that had been placed on the store as well because a carpenter hadn't been paid.

When I moved over to social media, I read a bunch of online complaints that local authors had given her books on consignment, and even though they had sold, the authors weren't getting paid for them. She also ran a series of workshops for aspiring writers, and several attendees had been unhappy with the harsh comments she had provided for their manuscripts.

It was clear she wasn't a very nice person—but then, I'd figured that out within a couple of minutes of meeting her. However, there was a big leap between being a bitch, as Mariana had called her, and pissing someone off enough to get murdered.

I wasn't even tempted to hack into her bank account or anywhere else. Rick was already investigating her death, and I trusted him to bring her justice.

# Chapter 6
## *Affaire De Coeur*

Sunday morning I checked my emails on my phone as I walked Rochester. The earliest one was from Jamie Quattrone, composed and sent in the middle of the night. Who was the student, he wanted to know?

I used my thumbs to tap out a response as Rochester nosed a magnolia tree coming into bud. "Darlene Giordano," I wrote. "Did you know her?"

His response popped back as Rochester and I were returning to the house. "That's a blast from the past," he wrote. "Sure, I'll talk to you. Join me for a cocktail this afternoon at four?"

I agreed. I fed Rochester his breakfast and then microwaved a couple of grocery store croissants for my own meal, slathered with strawberry jam from Styer's market. I realized with a laugh that I was just as pompous in my food sourcing as the Brown Dog Café; no supermarket jam for me.

By the time Lili joined me, I had mapped out an agenda for the day. I knew she had been wanting to see a photo exhibit at the Museum of Modern Art's PS1 facility in Queens. I thought I could browse through the exhibit with her, then leave her there for a longer look while I dropped in on Jamie Quattrone in Brooklyn.

They were open from twelve to six, which gave me about an hour and a half with Quattrone before I had to pick her up. "How does that work for you?" I asked.

"You know, I'd rather come with you to meet Quattrone, if you don't mind. I loved *The Art of the Scam*. He really captured the life of gallerists in SoHo in the 1970s. I think it would be cool to hear some of his stories—after he tells you about Darlene, of course."

"Sure. And then maybe we can have dinner at Donatello's." Donatello Nobatti was a celebrity chef and a friend of Lili's from her photojournalism days.

"He lost his lease on West 45$^{th}$," she said. "He relocated to Dumbo. So that should be perfect."

"I'm not surprised. He was too publicity-shy for his own good." We'd even made jokes about him—that his slogan ought to be 'if you like Donatello's food, don't tell nobody.'

Dumbo was my favorite neighborhood name in the city. It stood for Down Under the Manhattan Bridge Overpass, and it stretched along the Brooklyn waterfront in an area of old brick warehouses converted into trendy shops and restaurants. It wasn't a surprise that Donatello Nobatti had moved his restaurant there.

We ended up going to the museum first anyway, and I loved the way Lili observed the photographs, stepping back first to get the broad perspective, then zeroing in on certain details. I had learned about photography while living with her, but I was still somewhat of a Philistine—I liked pretty pictures.

"Which images made an impression on you?" Lili asked, as we walked back out to the car.

"That one of the gorge," I said. "I know it's supposed to be impressive because of the angle—I mean, he must have had to do some climbing and figuring to get the whole gorge in that way, from top to bottom, and still have you notice the individual trees and boulders. But it just made me think of suicide."

She stopped. "Suicide? Really?" A delivery truck rattled down the narrow street beside us, catching the leaves of the overhanging trees.

"Not me," I said. "But I keep thinking about these kids and their pills and killing themselves, either all at once or slowly."

She threaded her arm in mine. "Let's hope that Jamie Quattrone is more upbeat." Then she groaned. "But of course, we're there to talk about a woman who was murdered."

"Welcome to my world."

The Clock Tower was an impressive building of about a dozen stories, facing the East River and the towers of Manhattan. It was almost, but not quite, at the river's edge, separated by a children's park and a pebbled beach, though I couldn't imagine who would go swimming in the East River.

Quattrone's apartment was a couple of floors below the clock tower itself, and had broad arched windows that looked out at Manhattan. He was a heavyset fellow with carefully groomed gray hair, and he greeted us as if we were old friends. When Lili introduced herself she was very pleased that he knew some of her wartime work, which he called "very impressive."

"Can I offer you a French Manhattan?" he said. "That's my favorite drink right now. Cognac, vermouth, Cointreau, and a dash of bitters."

I looked at Lili and she smiled. "Sounds delightful," I said.

We marveled at the view while he mixed a pitcher. "You can almost see where Tor and I lived on the Lower East Side," I said. "See that mini-storage? Walk about three blocks in from the river."

"You were a Manhattanite?" Quattrone asked, as he brought a tray of coupe glasses to us, filled with a glowing orange mixture and a maraschino cherry nestled at the bottom.

"I went to graduate school in English at Columbia," I said, as I took a glass. "Then my friend Tor Svenson and I moved down there as we got our feet under us. I believe you know his wife, Sherri? The Realtor?"

"Of course, delightful woman." He sat in an overstuffed armchair and motioned us to sit across from him. "A shark, as well. She negotiated a very good deal for me."

He took a sip of his drink and sighed with pleasure. "But you didn't come to talk about real estate. You said you knew Darlene Giordano?"

"Only briefly," I said. I sipped my drink to fortify myself for what was to come. It was sublime.

"Darlene ran a small bookstore in the town where we live now, Stewart's Crossing, in Bucks County."

"I spent many a happy hour in New Hope," he said, naming the next big town up the river. "Literally."

"I went into the store last weekend to look for a book, and I found Darlene's body in her office. It was very upsetting, as you can imagine, and I ... I just wanted to know more about her as a person, when she was alive. I read in a profile of her that she'd studied with you at City College."

"It was an *affaire de coeur*," he said, sitting back in his chair. "She was in my senior fiction seminar and she was quite talented, for someone so young. I met her several times to go over her works, and, well, then, you know how these things happen."

I didn't, really. So far in my educational career I had managed to keep my hands off my students. Lili had married one of her professors when she was still an undergrad, but she said now that she regretted that affair. "Was she attractive, back then?"

He laughed. "I assume you're saying she wasn't anymore. I remember she had lovely blonde hair, in ripples like waves of the sea. We had a pleasant time together for the rest of her senior year, and then I sent her off to Iowa with a glowing recommendation."

"Did you keep in touch with her?"

He sipped his cocktail. "I read her work occasionally in literary magazines. I might have dropped her a note now and then. I even helped her find an agent for her thesis, a collection of stories, but those were out of fashion at the time. Everyone wanted novels then, you see. I had just published *The Art of the Scam*, and I encouraged her to stretch her imagination, write something more than a literary bauble. Something with heart, something with meat."

Beside me, I noticed Lili sitting forward, enraptured with his mellifluous voice. "And did she?" I asked.

"She had this damn fool idea about moving to an Indian reservation. She thought she'd write a great novel about abandoned, disenfranchised people yearning to transcend the bonds of their circumstance."

He let that hang in the air for a moment, then added, "A bunch of nonsense, if you want my opinion. What did a blonde from Queens know about any of that? I told her to come back to the city, get a job in publishing, write something big and trashy and adventurous."

"Like your works," Lili said, and I nearly choked on my drink.

"Exactly. I know my reputation, my dear. I tagged onto Norman's wagon, taking the headlines, adding a bit of literary spin. I can still put together a sentence to make your heart break. But Indians? Who wanted to read about them when there were captains of industry to make books out of?"

I remembered the phrase from one of Tom Wolfe's books. "Did you ever hear from her after that?"

"She did try to come back to the city after a year there, tail between her legs. But I was married then and I couldn't do much for her. She was quite resentful—but the bloom was off the rose, and there were lots of talented MFAs in line after her, each of them saying 'please, sir, I want some recognition.'"

He shook his head. "Too bad about her dying, though. I must have one of her stories here somewhere." He motioned to the shelves of books and literary journals which lined two walls. "I'll have to dig it out and read it again in her memory."

We chatted for a while longer, hearing a salacious story about Norman Mailer and another about a photographer Lili worshiped, then declined the offer of a second round of drinks and thanked him for his time.

In the elevator, Lili said, "We can walk to Donatello's from here. I looked up his new address and it's only a few blocks."

I wanted to ask her opinion of Quattrone, but he'd led her toward a sensitive subject, her first marriage, and I knew I had to wait for her to bring it up.

"Do you think she was happy?" she asked, as we walked outside.

There was a chill wind blowing in off the East River, and I buttoned up my coat. "Darlene, you mean? When she was young and talented?"

"Well, we clearly saw she was miserable at the time she died."

"I think I'd be," I said, choosing my words carefully. "Having a man as renowned as Quattrone recognize and celebrate my talent."

"He did think I was talented, you know, Adriano."

"I'm sure he did."

"It wasn't just that I was young and attractive and foolish in my choice of men."

I stopped and turned to her. "Do you think that Quattrone was wrong in sleeping with her when she was his student?"

"Of course. It's a terrible breach of academic ethics. And Adriano was wrong to romance me when I was barely out of my teens, and then marry me as if it would make up for what he'd done wrong. I was..." She shook her head. "I was sure that marrying him was wrong, but I didn't see any other future for myself."

"At least not then."

She smiled. "No, not then, and not for a while after."

She started walking again, and I followed her to the restaurant, whose homestyle brick walls and photos of famous Italians belied Donatello Nobatti's talent for cooking. We had a wonderful meal, talking about Quattrone's apartment, Lili's student portfolios, even what a rascal Brody had turned into.

It wasn't until we were in the car on our way back to Stewart's

Crossing that Lili said, "I like to think I learned something from my marriages."

"What's that?"

"I married both Adriano and Philip for the wrong reasons. I was looking for a man like my father, who would protect me and give my life some direction, some meaning."

I focused on driving. I had to find the entrance to I-278 toward the Verrazzano Narrows Bridge. As we approached the highway, Lili turned to me. "I realized I was looking for the wrong characteristics of my father."

I made my turn, and safe on the highway, said, "What were the right ones?"

"The ones I found in you. Kind, generous, loving. Giving me the freedom to be the best version of myself."

She leaned over and kissed my cheek. "Thanks."

# Chapter 7
## *Integrated Response*

Monday afternoon I met with the student suicide committee, though of course it wasn't called that. This was academia, after all, and so we had Student Engagement, Student Success, and Student Outreach offices. At a glance you'd be hard-pressed to figure out what any of them actually did. It didn't help that we'd just reorganized, moving a bunch of people around to new titles.

I had referred a student to Student Outreach the semester before, when his performance in my class deteriorated rapidly halfway as the term headed toward completion. He stopped making online discussion posts and stopped coming to class, and I called him to find out why.

It was difficult to get him to confide at first, but eventually he told me that he had come out to his parents at his twenty-first birthday, in early November. They had been paying his tuition, his dorm fees and his bookstore bill, but all that stopped immediately. He had housing only until December.

He had gone through some depression at first, he said, and stayed in bed for the first couple of weeks after the incident. He had so much to face that he said he just wanted to burrow under the covers.

He had no part-time job so when the money from his parents ran out, he had to sell his laptop to a fellow student to pay his cell phone bill. He didn't know where he would go when he had to leave the dorm, especially as he had no money for tuition, food and lodging in the spring term.

I convinced him to meet me at the campus library, and I brought along pamphlets from various student services. Eventually he let me walk him over to the building where all student services were house. A week later, he submitted his final paper, with a note that the Outreach staff had found him a part-time job, a room in a shared house in Leighville, and a combination of scholarships and student loans to pay his spring tuition.

I was so happy for him that I sent him a gift card for use at the big warehouse store outside Leighville, with a note that I hoped he could get some food there that would tide him through the holidays.

I had kept in touch with him since then via email. With the help of some friends, and the Outreach office, he was staying positive. I was very glad that the big blow he'd received hadn't led him to dropping out, addiction or suicide. I made a note to ask him if he'd be willing to speak to a group of students about his experience.

The committee met in a classroom on the top floor of Blair Hall, which housed the English Department. Tall, gothic-arched windows along one side let in natural light, supplemented on gray days by fluorescent lights hung on pendants around the room. A rich wooden wainscoting ran around the perimeter of the room, a legacy of Eastern's long history of deep-pocket alumni.

Because we weren't quite sure what our mission was, our committee's first task was to choose our own name and what we thought we were supposed to be doing. The chair was my friend Jackie Conrad from the Department of Natural Sciences, where she taught anatomy and physiology. She was still wearing her white lab coat and her blonde curls spilled over the collar. "Student Spirit Committee?" she suggested.

"Sounds like we're going to be out on Fields Green cheering with pom-poms," said the man next to me, a reed-thin professor from Philosophy named Ewan Garrett.

"Why don't we start with our purpose, and then come up with a name based on what we want to achieve?" I asked. When there was general assent, I continued.

"The way I understood President Babson in my five-minute meeting with him, he's worried that the pressure students are under could lead them to suicide. For example, athletes who feel the need to perform on the field in order to maintain their scholarships may turn to drugs to allow them to push past the pain, like Tyler Benjamin, and then that abuse could lead to suicide."

Eve Kinsman, a short, stocky woman who coached women's lacrosse and field hockey, interrupted me. "We're not just talking about athletes."

"I agree," I continued. "That was just the first of my points." I smiled at her. "We've got all kinds of students who could feel the pressure to perform, from legacies who don't want to disappoint their families to brilliant students with a particular pain point when it comes to a subject. Students who are the first in their families to go to college, and don't have anyone to turn to when they need academic advice."

"It seems like all these issues are being addressed individually," the last member of the committee said. He was the oldest among us, a senior professor from the History Department named Franklin Stone.

"You're both right," Jackie said. "Many different kinds of students are under pressure, and Eastern provides individualized support. But what if a student has problems in several areas?"

"The coaches can provide medical and therapeutic help and referrals to academic support services to athletes who are having problems," Coach Kinsman added.

"Do you monitor whether they take advantage of those resources?" Professor Garrett asked. "I know when I send a student for help on a paper, if I get a revised paper back with a stamp from the tutors, he or she did what I suggested. But if I don't..."

"The athletic staff could all do a better job of following up on individual students," Coach Kinsman admitted. "But we have a lot of kids to look after, and they have a lot of problems."

There was a general assent around the room. I thought for a moment of Darlene Nowak, back when she was in school at City College. What had driven her to an affair with a professor? Was it a need for love, or recognition?

"There are also emotional issues involved," I said. "Students who don't know how to live communally, who develop inappropriate crushes."

"I get a fair number who need some mothering," Jackie said. "Fortunately, with two of my own I can manage that. But I I know other professors who are frightened they'll get charged with inappropriate behavior if they get too close to a student."

"It seems like we need a more integrated response system," I said. "Managed by someone in advising who knows how to handle students with emotional needs as well as academic or physical ones."

"I think Steve has given us our committee title," Jackie said. "The Integrated Response Committee."

There was general consensus, and Jackie reminded us that President Babson had chosen us all for this committee. "We all must have particular skills he wants us to use. Why do you each think you were chosen for this committee? What you can contribute?"

She leaned forward. "I'm here because science courses are a particular pressure point for many students, and because I understand the chemical dependency issues that can arise in students." She looked at Coach Kinsman. "Eve?"

She was there to represent athletics, while Franklin Stone was to be our elder statesman, and Ewan Garrett was there because he was in his first year at Eastern and he could bring a fresh perspective.

He took a deep breath. "And I believe I'm here because I had Tyler Benjamin in my introduction to philosophy class in the fall."

*Dog Willing*

We all turned to look at him. "Did you know him well?" Jackie asked.

"I wish I had. I taught a lot while I was in graduate school, but never more than two classes a term. I didn't think I'd have trouble shifting to four classes when I got here, because my thesis was finished, and all I'd have to do on the side was polish up chapters for publication."

"Ah, the naivety of new faculty," Stone said. "How many students did you have between those four classes?"

"Two sections of intro and two sections of ethics. Thirty students in each."

"That's a hundred twenty students," I said. My experience had been like Garrett's, never teaching more than two sections of freshman comp or business writing at once. "How did you manage?"

"I was overwhelmed," Evan admitted. "The department chair gave me a standard syllabus for each class and I didn't have time to customize. I know I'm preaching to the choir here, but I had to create lesson plans for each course, twice a week, read and grade discussion posts, and grade papers. And my office hours were filled with students – either those with genuine interest who wanted to discuss the topics further, or those who were floundering and needed personal help."

"Which category did Tyler Benjamin fit into?" I asked.

"Neither. He was in the intro class, and he wrote clear, well-thought out answers to the discussion questions. He only wrote one paper, and it was very generic." He shook his head. "I guarantee you, after his suicide I went back over every word he wrote, looking for evidence that something was wrong."

"Do you run your discussion posts through the plagiarism software?" Eve asked.

"I didn't know you could do that. I thought it was only for papers?"

"It's trickier, because you have to do it one post at a time. I only do it when I suspect plagiarism." She sighed. "I'm an athlete, and a coach, and I hate to tar my own people with a broad brush, but those discussion posts are a loophole students can exploit. You get those questions direct from the publisher, don't you?"

Ewan nodded. "I haven't had time to create my own."

"An enterprising student can get hold of some good answers to those questions, and then pass them around. He ran track, so I wouldn't be surprised if someone on the team shared those answers with him."

Ewan bent over and put his head in his hands. "I never knew anything about him."

"It happens," Jackie said kindly. "If you are interested in a medical career, and you fail one of my courses, you might as well change your major. Medical schools, nursing schools—they use a single failure in a class like anatomy and physiology a way to cull the herd. I often have students who struggle the whole term, and never come to me for help until right before the final, when they tell me their parents will kill them if they don't get into med school."

She smiled. "I don't think they mean it literally. I have to have serious talks with them about what they really do well at and how they can shift their parents' expectations. And for every one who comes to me, there are at least two who take the F and try again and keep falling farther and farther behind. There's only so much we can do."

She looked at me. "Steve? What about you? Why do you think you're on this committee?"

I considered what I wanted to say, and then decided that honesty and openness were the best policies. "I run the Friar Lake Conference Center, and I teach the occasional course in the English Department as an adjunct. I know President Babson wants us to use Friar Lake to bring together different stakeholders for some of our discussions and programs."

I took a deep breath. "But more than that, I think I'm here because President Babson knows the problems I've encountered in my life, and how I've worked to overcome them, and his belief in me has been a major factor in how I rebuilt my life after my wife miscarried, my marriage ended, and I served a prison term for computer hacking."

The rest of the room was quiet. Mine certainly wasn't the standard path to a job in academia. "I want to use what I learned in overcoming stress to help us provide the right kind of guidance for our students."

"I appreciate your honesty, Steve," Franklin Stone said after a moment. "And even an old fossil like me has faced down some problems. I'm sure we can all help in that regard."

# Chapter 8
## *Shining Armor*

That evening, I took Rochester past the dog park in River Bend. Perhaps because I'd left him alone while I went to Eastern for the committee meeting, he seemed over-excited, and I hoped a good run would calm him down.

Arielle was standing by a tree, her hands in her pockets, but as soon as she saw me she hurried over. I let Rochester go run with Emma and turned to Arielle. She was pale, and her eyes had a haunted look.

"The police came to talk to me again this afternoon after I got Brandon and Sophia home from school. It looks like Darlene Nowak was murdered."

"Do they know how?"

She shook his head. "The detective wouldn't say, but he kept asking questions about the *croque monsieur* she was eating when she died. How did I make it? What were the ingredients? Did I make it specially for her? Did I put the wrong kind of mushrooms in?"

A breeze swept through the park, shaking the baby buds on the oaks and maples. I pulled down the sleeves of my sweater. "Which detective was it? Stemper or Vickers?"

She pulled a card from her pocket. "Detective Richard Stemper. Do you know him?"

I nodded my head. "We went to Pennsbury High together, and we got to be friends after I came back to Stewart's Crossing. You don't have to worry. He's a smart guy and he knows his job. He won't jump to any conclusions."

She looked at me. "Wait a second. Didn't you work with the police when the property manager was murdered?"

An owl swooped past us and we watched as it grabbed a tiny mouse in its talons, then took flight over the rooftops of River Bend.

"I wouldn't say I worked with the police," I said. "Rick and I know each other, like I said, and I told him some of the things going on here in River Bend."

I didn't want to tell her how many crimes Rochester and I had helped Rick with. He was the police detective, after all, and I did believe in his intelligence and his competence. It's just that sometimes Rochester had been able to nose out a clue or two for him.

"Then you have to help me." She took my hand, and hers were slim, bony and cold. "My relationship with Pierre is terrible, and if the police arrest me for something I didn't do, he'll try to take Brandon and Sophia from me. I can't lose my kids. It'll kill me."

By then I'd gotten a good idea how dramatic Arielle was, but I understood her passion. If either of the babies that my ex had miscarried had come to term, I was sure I'd feel the same.

I blew out a long breath. Lili had often compared me to one of those medieval knights, who felt an obligation to help a fair maiden in trouble. Arielle was dark-haired, not fair, yet she was clearly in trouble.

"How well did you know Darlene Nowak?" I asked.

Another chill breeze swept through the dog park and Arielle shivered. "Not at all! That's what's so crazy."

"You seemed to know who she was when she came out to complain."

She looked across the park to where Rochester and Emma were

romping. "We've been going to that center for a couple of months now and she always comes out and makes problems."

There was something about the way that Arielle wouldn't meet my eyes that made me believe there was something more to the story. "And?"

She sighed, and looked back at me. "And she runs these workshops for writers, like I told you."

"You want to write a novel?"

"Not me, Sophia. Darlene had this creative writing workshop for kids, and I thought it might be good for Sophia. Writing is her weak spot—she can read and talk a mile a minute but she has trouble putting her ideas into words on the page. When Darlene started her classes, she bragged about having literary credentials, and of course this was before we started going to the center with the food trucks. I took her to Darlene's class hoping she could help."

"And did she?"

Arielle shook her head violently, her bob sweeping. "She made it worse. I wasn't there, you know, but Sophia told me Darlene yelled at her when she couldn't get started on her story. Told her she was illiterate. She had the nerve to ask if Sophia was even American."

Her eyes flashed at me. "She was born at St. Francis Hospital in Trenton. Of course she's an American!"

I'd been born in that same hospital. "You took her there that one time?" I asked.

"You think I'd take her back after that? For two weeks afterward I couldn't get Sophia to write as much as a grocery list. What an awful woman!"

I had taught a youth workshop in East Harlem in the course of my MA, so I knew that you had to be especially delicate when it came to kids, to encourage them even when there was little positive to say.

Darlene had spent a year on an Indian reservation. Had she been harsh to her students there, and been asked to leave? I wouldn't be surprised.

Rochester and Emma came rushing back to us then, and we both had to leave the dog park. As I walked home, I thought about what Arielle had told me. She had a two-part motive to kill Darlene Nowak. Darlene was threatening the food truck business, and she had hurt Arielle's daughter, Sophia. But was either of those strong enough to take someone's life? And could Arielle have prepared something deadly in the short term after Otto made his offer?

I stopped on the way home and picked up the mail, which I left lying on the coffee table in the living room. I fed Rochester dinner, and Lili and I ate, and then he seemed to have an excess of energy—he kept romping around the living room, and eventually his big foofy tail swept the mail off the coffee table.

There wasn't much there except a flyer from the local hospital reminding us that spring brought with it a host of health problems, from allergies to new growth of poison ivy. The word poison reminded me that the police thought Darlene Nowak had been murdered. That meant something had been placed in or on her food that caused her death.

Could it have been an allergen? My cousin's son was very sensitive to peanuts, and when he came in touch with them, even just the dust they left behind, his throat swelled and he broke out in hives. I hadn't seen any evidence of hives on Darlene Nowak's face, but she still might have had a reaction to something in the *croque monsieur*. I didn't believe that Arielle would have had poisoned mushrooms on hand in her food truck. Could you be allergic to kale? Maybe Darlene was lactose intolerant. But why eat something rich in melted cheese, then?

I sat on the couch, and Rochester clambered up beside me and rested his head in my lap. Why would Darlene have vomited, though? That indicated to me that something had irritated her stomach. A poison? I found it hard to believe that Arielle could have poisoned Darlene's sandwich, but I didn't really know her, just that she was a nice woman with a friendly dog. That shouldn't remove her from suspicion.

Rochester was not happy when I stood up and fetched my laptop. I sat at the dining room table and looked for a poison that would cause vomiting and result in a quick death. It was a complicated thing to look for, because I had no access to any of Nowak's medical records. I went through a bunch of different choices, including arsenic. When swallowed, it caused severe gastric distress, burning esophageal pain, vomiting, and diarrhea with blood.

With a high enough dose, death occurred quickly. Would the police test Darlene's blood for arsenic? I knew from past experience that in an unexplained death, the medical examiner would run a series of tests, but according to what I read, it was possible that an autopsy would find only an inflamed stomach and possibly a trace of arsenic in the digestive tract. Was that enough to consider her death a murder?

I kept looking, and stumbled onto an article about opioid abuse. Many people who took pain pills like hydrocodone, oxycodone, morphine, fentanyl, and codeine were at risk for fatal overdoses. According to the article, more people were dying in the United States from opioid painkiller overdoses than from heroin and cocaine combined.

Could someone have slipped some opioids into Darlene Nowak's food? How easy would that be? I kept searching, skipping around through databases and websites and eventually discovered that fentanyl tablets could be ground up and scattered in the food Darlene was eating, causing the vomiting and quick death she had experienced. But it was dangerous to handle—would Arielle have known how to get it into the food without touching it or inhaling it herself?

The articles I read made it seem disturbingly easy to get hold of drugs like fentanyl, and I remembered what Arielle had said, that she was worried her son was using drugs. If he was, and he had fentanyl around, could his mother have confiscated it and used it to kill Darlene Nowak? Her biggest fear was losing custody of her kids, so I doubted she'd risk everything that mattered to her to punish a woman for a series of small irritations.

Once again, I realized I was spinning out stories without much proof. But it was clear I needed to know more about the food truck culture, and what the vendors thought of Nowak, before I made any more guesses. I checked online to see when and where the next food truck rally would be.

The next one was on Wednesday evening, in the parking lot of Pennsbury High in Fairless Hills, the school Rick and I had attended. I thought it might be useful to go over there and talk more to the food vendors, and I went upstairs to find Lili in the office.

I leaned against the door and told her I had agreed to help Arielle Brodeur.

She swiveled the chair around to face me. "I've said it before, and I'll say it again. You are a knight in shining armor, ready to help any damsel in distress. It's one of the many things I love about you."

"You don't mind if I go snooping again?"

"How can I mind, when it's so much a part of who you are? Just be careful. Don't irritate someone and then accept food from them."

I laughed. "I'll try not to."

# Chapter 9
## *Kids and Dogs*

The next morning I called Rick as I was taking Rochester for his morning walk. I knew I wouldn't wake him—his shift started at eight, and he was often at his desk even earlier.

"Hey, you want to meet for a beer at the Drunken Hessian tonight?" I asked, when he answered. It was one of the oldest bars in Bucks County, in the middle of downtown Stewart's Crossing. Rick and I had spent many hours there together since my return.

"For what reason?"

"You're my best friend, and I haven't seen you for a while." In the background I heard the chatter of other cops, a call coming in on the police radio. It reminded me of the distance between us. Solving the murder of Darlene Nowak was Rick's job, not mine.

"You saw me on Saturday afternoon, remember? At the food truck rally?" Someone in the station laughed very loud, and I had the sense that Rick turned the phone away from the noise.

"Fine. Arielle Brodeur's dog Emma likes to play with Rochester, and we saw them yesterday at the dog park in River Bend."

"And now you want to pump me for information on my case."

"Well, when you put it like that," I said defensively. "Yes."

He laughed. "At least we can be honest with each other. And I'm interested in some more insight into this woman. Six-thirty? First round's on you."

I agreed.

When I got to work, I found that Ewan Garrett, the philosophy professor, had taken notes on our committee meeting and forwarded them to all of us. For a moment I felt blessed that I was not on the tenure track at Eastern, struggling to make a good impression wherever I went, hoping each effort would somehow lead to the nirvana of a lifetime job teaching something I loved.

I didn't feel strongly enough about teaching for that. I'd figured that out when I was in graduate school at Columbia, and I taught a couple of sessions of freshman comp as part of my aid package. I enjoyed the contact with students, and still did. I wasn't excited by grading papers, but I didn't mind when I only taught one class at a time. I thought that facing a lifetime of teaching the same material, grading the same papers, and sitting through endless college meetings would drive me insane.

At least I only had to handle part of that.

Garrett's notes were clear and concise, and he had added a few thoughts of his own when he sent what he had written down. I spent some time that morning composing a response to the committee. I suggested that Friar Lake was a great place for off-campus seminars, both for faculty and at-risk students. To be most effective, though, we would have to come up with content to deliver, and then figure out who our target audience was. I reminded them that we had a kitchen on-site, so serving food would be a big draw, and that if I filed the right forms, I could get a shuttle bus driver from the campus to bring students out from Eastern if they didn't have their own transportation.

When I went to Eastern, the only way I had to get around campus was on foot or on my bike. Today's kids, however, were a lot more spoiled. Even though they might live on campus and eat in the dining hall, their parents gave them cars, and the student lots behind the dorms were always full. When I taught, I often heard students chat about heading to New York or Philadelphia over the weekend. Those whose parents had the deepest pockets stayed over in hotels, ate in high-end restaurants, even bought day passes to fancy spas and gyms.

I wondered if that disposable income led to them being able to buy drugs, too. I knew a cop on the Leighville force, Tony Rinaldi, and he had told me in the past that so far his department had been able to keep a lid on outside drug dealers. That didn't count what students brought in on their own, from home or their city trips, and the casual trade between them.

Tyler Benjamin was a case in point. He had begun using opiates for pain, prescribed by his family physician. That doctor kept renewing prescriptions even when Tyler was a thousand miles from home at Eastern. From an article I'd read, I learned that none of his classmates or teammates were willing to admit supplying him or knowing if he had an on-campus dealer.

His cross-country coach had known he was struggling, and given him regular pep talks, though like Ewan Garrett he had a lot of athletes to work with.

Eastern prided itself on being a very good small college, one where we had a high faculty-student ratio, but we had always focused on academics. We had a solid student health facility, and professors were required to maintain regular office hours.

Somehow, though, we had failed Tyler. Ewan had been too new, and too busy, to spot the boy's problems. What about his other professors? A junior like Tyler had to take four classes a term. Were his teammates propping him up, providing him with essays and test answers, so that his professors wouldn't notice?

And who had that benefited, in the end?

I was too agitated to sit in my office, so I took Rochester out for a late morning walk. The weather had taken a turn for the better, and being out in nature soothed me. I spotted a blue jay flitting through the trees, and saw the first tendrils of daffodils poking up in a bed in front of the chapel, where we held big functions.

I couldn't do anything more for Tyler, but I could do my best with the committee to help Eastern intervene with students like him in the future.

I spent the rest of the day reviewing invoices from suppliers, revising advertising copy about an upcoming seminar, and answering emails. I took Rochester home, fed and walked him, then drove over to the Drunken Hessian.

Rick was my best friend, and we didn't have as much time to hang out together as we had when we'd first connected, when I recognized him in line at Gail's Chocolate Ear café and we began hanging out together. He was the one who had asked me to look after Rochester when my next-door-neighbor had been killed.

The few days until he was able to contact Caroline's next of kin stretched on, and Rochester became my permanent companion. Within six months Rick had found an Australian Shepherd he called Rascal at the Bucks County SPCA in New Hope, and we spent hours every week together playing with and exercising the dogs.

Then I met Lili, and Rick started coaching a Pop Warner football team, where he met Tamsen Morgan, his girlfriend. We didn't have as much guy time anymore, and I missed that.

I pulled into the parking lot. The Drunken Hessian was a bar slash tourist trap in the center of Stewart's Crossing. The sign on the pole beside the two-story building depicted one of the Hessian soldiers whom Washington had surprised at Trenton on Christmas day, looking like he'd had quite a few too many. A plaque on the ground said that an inn of some kind had been on that spot since the Revolutionary War.

Inside, it looked like the décor hadn't much changed, except for the introduction of indoor plumbing. I walked into the dim bar and grabbed a booth along the side wall. I did believe that I had been helpful to Rick on a couple of cases, and that maybe I could help him out this time, too. I wanted to ask him about the case he had against Arielle Brodeur, but I also wanted to know what else was going on in his life. He had started spending the occasional overnight at Tamsen's house. How was that going? Was her son Justin still getting along with Rascal?

I was about to ask about those things when Rick swung into the booth across from me and said, "I know what you're going to ask, and the answer is yes."

I was confused. Yes to which question?

"Don't play dumb. You want to know if there was something deadly in that bag that Rochester found."

He signaled to the waitress and we ordered a pair of Dogfish Head Flesh and Blood IPA, brewed not far away from us in Delaware with a mix of lemon flesh and blood orange juice. Rick had a perverse liking for it, though it was a bit summery for April. Must be a cop thing, going for the gruesomeness of the name.

"Honestly?" I asked. "I was going to lead off with you and Tamsen, or Justin and Rascal."

"You're learning manners. Must be Lili's influence." He laughed. "Tamsen and I are fine. I went over there Saturday night after I got off duty, and spent the night, and all day Sunday. Justin and Rascal are still getting along like a house on fire—both of them have so much energy, and they seem to wear out about the same time."

The waitress brought our beers, and we ordered burgers and fries. We knocked our bottles together. "To kids and dogs," I toasted.

"Rascal's the perfect breed for Tamsen, too," he said. "You know, with Ryan dying so young and leaving the two of them on their own, Tam's been a bit overprotective of the boy."

"Can't blame her for worrying about losing him." I thought about Arielle, and her desire to retain custody of Brandon and Sophia.

"I know. But with Rascal, she's willing to let him go for long runs around the neighborhood, because she knows Rascal will keep him out of trouble."

He looked at me. "So. What kind of trouble have you been getting into?"

"Nothing much. We've got a new initiative at Eastern, to do something about all the stress college students have."

"Get 'em all dogs," Rick said. "Aussies and sheepdogs to keep them out of trouble and raise their endorphins."

"I'll add that to our list. Maybe I could loan Rochester out to the counseling office to get kids calmer."

"Rochester will jump all over them and lick them to death. I'm not sure you want that in a counseling office."

We sipped our beers for a moment. "Back to my initial comment. I sent the baggie off to the lab in Doylestown to be tested and the contents came back."

"Was it some kind of opiate?"

"I'll answer that in a second. First, there's a difference between opiates and opioids. You know what that is?"

"As I recall we didn't cover that in chemistry." That was the high school class where Rick and I had first gotten to know each other.

"Opiates are drugs that are naturally derived from the opium poppy plant, like heroin, morphine and codeine. Those are the ones they warned us about back in high school health class, along with marijuana, of course." He picked up his beer and took another sip. I wondered how many people in the Drunken Hessian knew what he was talking about—and how many of them had personal experience with the drugs.

"And opioids?" I asked.

"That's a broader term that refers to anything that binds to the part of brain that controls pain, reward, and addiction. Natural opiates are opioids, but so are synthetic drugs like Vicodin and OxyContin."

The server brought our burgers, and I took a bite of mine. "What was in the baggie?"

"Fentanyl powder. Fentanyl is one of those synthetic opioids, and it's fifty to one hundred times more potent than morphine. You're lucky you didn't touch the stuff in that baggie. A cop in Ohio got some fentanyl powder on his uniform while making a bust, and when he brushed it off with his finger he went into overdose."

It certainly didn't seem like the kind of risk a loving mother like Arielle would take. "Was that the stuff that killed Darlene Nowak?"

"Right now I can't make the connection, but it's one of those cases where two plus two equals four. The powder in the baggie is the same stuff that was sprinkled on Mrs. Nowak's sandwich. But did the stuff that killed Mrs. Nowak come from that particular baggie? Our analysis isn't that sophisticated."

We ate, and drank, and we both thought for a while. "Any fingerprints on the baggie?" I asked after a while.

"Nope. Looks like someone used gloves, which isn't unusual in a food preparation environment like you had with all those trucks feeding people. Anybody could have used gloves to handle the food and no one would have a second thought about it."

"How do you connect that baggie to the sandwich?"

"We don't, at least not right now. I'm back to square one. Means, motive, opportunity."

"Do any of the people you spoke with on Saturday have criminal records for drug abuse?"

"Nope. But you can buy this stuff online, if you know where to look. I'm sure you've seen it in your forays into the dark web." The dark web, I had taught Rick long ago, was the part of the internet, unseen to ordinary users, where crime thrived.

"I'm mostly looking for hacking software when I dive in there." I didn't have to lie to Rick about my background. He knew that I'd been arrested for hacking and served my time, but that it was an addiction, and like any addiction, needed constant monitoring to make sure it did not get out of hand.

I satisfied my urges by keeping my hacking tools up to date. I couldn't carry out a major operation, like a distributed denial of service, where you harness innocent computers to flood a particular website with requests, causing it to go down. I no longer had the ability to break into heavily secured sites like banks and credit unions. But I could get into email servers, poorly protected company databases and so on.

Not that I did that anymore.

"Theoretically, could someone figure out if any of the people who had access to Mrs. Nowak's sandwich ordered fentanyl online?"

I took a deep breath. "I doubt it. From what I've read there are so many places you can order from, and without a few more clues it would be like looking for a heroin needle in a haystack."

"Clever."

"If you had a suspect, you could confiscate that person's computer and check their email and browser history. I could help you look through that, if you need."

He nodded. "Good to know. Right now, any one of them could have had the means to get the fentanyl."

"Then motive?" I asked. "You always say there are four motives for murder. Love, lust, lucre and loathing. Who loved Darlene Nowak?"

"No one, as far as I can tell. She was married once, when she was young, but divorced soon after that. Nothing I've found in examining her office and her home indicates anyone was lusting after her, either."

I finished my last fry and pushed the plate away. "She was a more lovable person when she was younger," I said. "Lili and I went up to Brooklyn on Sunday. We met this guy Darlene had an affair with when he was a professor and she was a student. Seems like she had a lot of promise as a literary star but never fulfilled it."

"There is an ex-husband," Rick said. "I looked him up and spoke to him. Bill Novak. Apparently another one of those artists with an MFA and great promise who never fulfilled it."

"Really?"

"He says that she married him when he was driving a cab, thinking that living with another artist would inspire her creativity. She agreed to support him for a year, and at the end of it he had his first show, at a gallery. He had taken some nude photos of her—artistic nudes, he says—and she didn't realize he'd exhibit them. She got pissed and divorced him."

"I'd have been pissed too, in her shoes."

"He ended up moving to the San Fernando Valley, outside LA, and doing that kind of work for a living."

"Really?"

"Yeah. Apparently at one point nearly 90% of legal porn came from there. He was sorry to hear she was dead, but hadn't been in touch with her for a long time."

I thought about that for a moment. Two young, promising artists, both derailed, But then, how many of Lili's students would end up as professional photographers? And who was to say that the kind of nudes in porn magazines weren't a kind of art, too?

I sipped my beer as those thoughts ran through my head.

"What about lucre?" Rick asked. "I looked up her Social Security records and I know she worked at a bunch of those Internet start-ups. Did she have a lot of money put aside?"

"I don't think so. The one place she worked that had a profitable IPO tanked a year later. And I did a bit of quick searching in public records and she owed money to her landlord and a contractor, and to a bunch of authors who gave her books on consignment. Apparently, she was very slow to pay those back."

"She owned a little house off Ferry Road, north of downtown, not worth much but mortgaged to the hilt. It's doubtful there are heirs out there expecting to inherit a bundle."

"Which leaves us with loathing," I said. "A lot of those food truck people didn't like her. I understand that every time they were at the shopping center she complained and raised a ruckus."

"There's a term I haven't heard in a long time," Rick said, smiling. "Raised a ruckus."

"Bitched and moaned, then."

"But is that enough of a motive to kill someone?" he asked. "I keep thinking there must be something more to her life. She was the kind of woman you wouldn't notice if you passed her on the street, but someone hated her enough to poison her."

He shook his head. "Which brings us to opportunity. The person with easiest access to that sandwich is the person who made it. Arielle Brodeur."

"But I saw that sandwich, pre-made and shrink-wrapped, on her shelf," I said. "She didn't start out the day knowing she was going to have an opportunity to poison Darlene Nowak. And she wouldn't leave a sandwich with poison out on the shelf because someone else might get it."

"How do you know that? If this woman complained every time they went to the center, maybe Mrs. Brodeur had that sandwich ready for the opportunity to give it to her."

I finished the last of my burger, which left a bad taste in my mouth. Could Arielle Brodeur be the kind of woman who would think that far in advance?

"You've talked to her," Rick said. "Do you think she has a reasonable motive? And remember, she may be a nice lady and great with dogs, but she could still be a cold-hearted killer. And the only way to clear somebody is usually to put all the information out up front."

"I know. And I don't know her all that well. We've talked, and I know she's going through a bad divorce, which is enough to stress any normal person. That food truck represents a chance to make a new life for herself and her kids, and anybody, like Darlene Nowak, who gets in the way, could be an obstacle she needs to remove."

He nodded. "It's not a big motive, but sometimes people's motivation to do the wrong thing can be awfully petty."

"There's one more thing, about her daughter." I explained about the writing workshop for children that Sophia Brodeur had attended. "When Arielle talked about how Mrs. Nowak upset Sophia, she was all mother lion protecting her cub. Again, I don't think it's a strong motive, but you never know."

Rick drained the last of his beer and motioned the server for a check. "This one's on me. I feel like I got more out of this session than you probably did."

"There's one more thing," I said. "There's another food truck rally tomorrow night, in the high school parking lot. I was thinking of going over there to talk to the other vendors. That all right with you?"

"Since when are you asking me for permission to nose around?" He laughed. "Sure. I was going to go myself but tryouts for Little League are coming up and I promised Justin I'd help him with his pitching and catching. Jerry Vickers might stop by, though."

"I'll be your eyes and ears then."

"Be careful what you eat. You don't want to ask too many questions and then have the vendor try to poison you, too."

"I'll only order something I can see made in front of me, and I won't ask any questions until I've eaten."

"Good man. I'd hate to see anything happen to you."

# Chapter 10
## *Spreadsheet*

It was mid-evening by the time I got home, and Lili and I sat together in the bedroom and watched a couple of episodes of a TV series we were streaming. I walked Rochester before bed, and then took him with me up to Friar Lake the next morning.

While he sat on the floor beside me and gnawed a bone filled with peanut butter, I put together a spreadsheet of each of the food truck vendors and workers. It wasn't easy; I had to rely on memory, and on the website that listed each of the trucks.

I began the way I had talked with Rick the night before, with columns titled Means, Motive and Opportunity. I also listed Opposing Arguments to make sure I looked at all angles.

The first suspect I listed was Arielle Brodeur. Under motive, I wrote "threat to business." Arielle needed her food truck to succeed, to make enough money to supplement what her ex paid her. If it failed, she'd have to take a job, one that might reduce the amount of time she could spend with Brandon and Sophia. In turn, that might amplify Pierre Brodeur's case for custody.

It was a stretch, but if Darlene Nowak was trying to hurt the food trucks, she was a threat to Arielle's goals. However, Darlene only wanted the trucks out of the way of her store. All her threats and complaints were aimed at moving the trucks, not shutting them down.

I created a second line under motive, and noted how Darlene had been mean to Sophia in the children's writing workshop. "Protective mom?" I wrote there. I had to admit that seeking revenge for someone who was mean to your kid was a fairly weak motive, especially if the cruelty was a one-time thing, but I knew people had killed for less.

Under Opposing Arguments, I noted that Arielle had a lot to lose if she was convicted of the murder—jail, the loss of her freedom and ceding custody of her kids to her ex. Those seemed a lot more powerful than the motives, and I was relieved. I hoped I was arguing on the side of the angels, but you never know.

She had the opportunity, because it was her croque monsieur that had the poison applied to it. I added that unless Arielle was really stupid, she wouldn't poison a dish that could be traced back to her so easily.

Then I came to means. Was Arielle taking pain killers for any reason? I recalled her saying something about Brandon getting moody, and she worried that he might be on drugs. Suppose she had found his stash, and used it on Darlene? It was a long shot, but I had to add it. I wondered how I could ask her if she'd ever taken opioids herself, or had them prescribed for one of her kids. I didn't think there was a diplomatic way, but I'd keep it in the back of my mind.

Rochester nudged me, and I remembered what Mark had said about vets dispensing similar pills. "Good idea, boy," I said, and rubbed his head. Then I added Emma, Arielle's dog, to the mix in case the lab had been prescribed with pain killers.

I was interrupted by a knock on the door to my office, and Rochester immediately jumped up and scrambled over to see Franklin Stone there.

"Rochester. Be nice," I said, as I stood up. "Hi, Professor Stone. Welcome to Friar Lake."

"Please, call me Franklin." He leaned down to pet Rochester's soft head. "Are you the assistant director here, Rochester?"

"He tends to think he's in charge. Come in, sit down. What brings you out here?"

Franklin wore khaki slacks and a green loden cloth jacket with leather elbow patches—the way professors had dressed back when I was an Eastern undergraduate. "I've been thinking about our committee and your offer to host some events out here. I thought I'd drop by and get the lay of the land."

"President Babson wanted to create a state-of-the-art conference center here, to expand Eastern's influence in the world, as well as to serve our students, faculty, staff and the local community. We've only been open two years, and we've made a good start on those goals."

I stood up. "Would you like a tour of the facilities?"

He agreed, and we walked outside. The air was sunny and crisp, and Rochester took off to chase a squirrel. I showed Franklin the chapel, the classrooms and the catering facilities, giving him tidbits of the facility's history as we went.

"I didn't know there was a monastery out here," he said. "I'm afraid my specialty is modern European history, so I've never paid much attention to the history all around us."

Rochester had given up on his squirrel and was sniffing around the base of a tree. "I grew up down the river in Stewart's Crossing. We learned Revolutionary War history on every field trip. Back then, there were farms and fields everywhere, and you could imagine redcoats lurking behind the next tree, or Washington gathered around a table with his top advisors plotting the Christmas eve attack on Trenton."

He stopped. "With the world changing around us so quickly, do you think we can really make an impact on students' lives?"

"Education helps us find our place. Eastern did that for me, and I think it still does."

"Sorry, I didn't mean in the macro sense. Of course I believe we have something to teach, and students have something to learn. I meant this committee. It seems like there are so many problems to address. How can we manage?"

"I was taught, here at Eastern, that the best way to approach a big problem is to break it down into smaller ones," I said. "Can we stop every student who wants to commit suicide from doing so? Sadly, I don't think so. But if we can help one of them, or two of them? Then it's worth our effort."

"I have been teaching here for nearly forty years," Franklin said. I was surprised; he didn't look that old. And that meant that he'd been there when I was an undergrad, though I had never known him or taken a class with him. "Maybe I'm getting jaded. I need young people like Ewan Garrett, and you, to remind me of what we can still achieve."

We started walking again. "How do you propose we break up this larger problem into smaller ones?" he asked.

"Students have always felt pressure to achieve, especially at a school like Eastern," I said. "If I recall correctly, in our freshman orientation we learned that nearly half of us had been valedictorians or salutatorians of our high school class. I had friends who were accustomed to getting straight A's who were devastated by a B."

"One of my colleagues in the Economics Department told me recently that some of the most prestigious companies that recruit here will only interview students in the top quarter of the class. And we're all familiar with how much more difficult it is to get into the top law and medical schools."

"That's one small problem," I said. "How do we reduce anxiety about performance? Other colleges have addressed that. At Brown, students can opt for conventional grading or satisfactory/no credit. There are no D grades and failures don't get marked on their records."

"And graduate programs don't like that. It makes students harder to quantify, and as we know, in many cases it's all about the numbers."

"You're right." I paused and watched Rochester romp ahead of us. "The biggest problem I think we face right now is the increased use of drugs, particularly opioids. In Tyler Benjamin's case drug use was a big contributing factor to his suicide."

"Oh, for the good old days of marijuana," Franklin said. "The worst thing that happened was that students came to class red-eyed and fell asleep."

I laughed. "That still happens, though many professors aren't quite as generous as you are about it."

"I lecture with the lights down and photos of historical sites and artifacts up on the screen," he said. "I know the effect can be somewhat soporific. But for the right kind of student it can bring history to life."

"How do we focus on drug use?" I asked, as we started to walk again. "Integrate the problem into the curriculum? I was an English major, and I vaguely remember that a lot of poets and writers used opium. We could discuss that with students, disabuse them of the romantic notion of using drugs."

"Something to think about, certainly. I'm sure the sciences could work something in, even my dusty discipline of history."

"And economics, and political science," I said.

We agreed to bring that up at our next meeting, and talked more as we wandered the property. Then Franklin thanked me for the tour, said goodbye to Rochester, and headed off to campus.

I went back into my office and returned to my spreadsheet, though ideas about opioid abuse and how to handle it kept dancing at the back of my brain.

The other person associated with Arielle's Cuisine de France was Arielle's assistant, Keenwa, who had called out sick that day, resulting in my stint at the register. Had she done so deliberately so she wouldn't be on site when Darlene was murdered?

I found a Yelp page where a reviewer mentioned "Keenwa Johnson was really helpful in explaining the menu." I looked further but couldn't find anything else about Keenwa, which was surprising because I thought she was a millennial, and I expected her to pop up all over social media.

I looked to Rochester for help. "Any ideas, puppy?"

He rolled over onto his side. "Not helping." But then I looked above him at a crude sign one of the neighbor's children had made as part of a fund-raising project. It was a piece of clay the size of a pawprint, with each toe indented. The kid had written ROCHSTER in crude letters.

Even though the name was misspelled, I bought it from the kid because I want to do anything I can to encourage kids to love dogs. Every time we were out walking and a kid asked, "Can I pet your dog?" I said yes, and showed him or her the right way to approach.

Too bad the kid couldn't spell.

Maybe I was making the same mistake. Was I spelling Keenwa wrong? I tried "Quinoa Johnson" and the only hit was for a man by that name who worked for an investment firm and had a lion as his Facebook profile picture.

I popped in "Johnson" and "Arielle's Cuisine de France," and someone named Kelly Artinae Johnson came up with a match to Arielle's food truck as her most recent place of work. I wondered why she used a different name—I was pretty sure Arielle had told me her mother had given her that name because she liked the sound of it.

Alarm bells began ringing in my head, so I logged into a database I used when I was interested in someone's criminal record. It was expensive and I didn't pay for it, using a password I had found on the dark web. Every time I checked it I felt unclean—but I couldn't say if that was because of the illicit password, or because of what I was able to learn.

While Keenwa had no criminal history, Kelly had a doozy of one, beginning with a sealed juvenile record. Since turning eighteen, she had been arrested on several first-degree misdemeanor charges for possession of a controlled substance, all of them dropped. I did some quick checking and figured those were probably for possession of marijuana in a quantity of less than twenty grams.

Those were no big deal. It was the still-pending charge that floored me, one of accessory after the fact in the commission of a capital crime. It took some more digging, but I discovered that Kelly Johnson had driven a boyfriend to the Greyhound station in Levittown, where she had bought him a ticket to New York in her name.

Said boyfriend, Isaiah "Crumple" Bidwell, was accused of three drug-related murders in Philadelphia.

According to the records I found, Kelly had pleaded innocent, unaware of why Crumple wanted to leave town. I figured it was after that incident that she'd changed her name to Keenwa, though I had no proof of that. It made me uncomfortable to discover that she'd lied to Arielle, and I debated whether I ought to reveal that information to her.

When I returned to Stewart's Crossing, I didn't have to lie about my criminal record. I had begun building up freelance writing clients I found online, and all those clients cared about was how well I could write and how fast I could turn around the work.

Then one day I drove up to Eastern to speak with the professor who taught my senior seminar in English. He remembered me, or at least pretended to, and since he was the chair of the department then he offered me the chance to teach a single freshman comp course that spring.

I impressed him, and then President Babson, and I had the chance to rebuild my life. How much tougher it must be for a young women without education and contacts.

It was a big step, of course, from buying a boyfriend a bus ticket, even if Keenwa was aware of what he was accused of, or what he had done, to committing murder herself. But the fact that Keenwa wasn't on site the day Darlene was killed smacked of creating an alibi to me.

I entered all the information I found on Keenwa/Kelly into my spreadsheet. Her motive? If Arielle's food truck had to shut down, it might be difficult for Keenwa to get another job, given her criminal record. She could have seen Darlene Nowak as a threat to her continued employment.

But again, the only thing Darlene threatened was the food truck rally at the shopping center. Not Arielle's entire business.

Means was a trickier entry. Even though she didn't work that day, Keenwa was familiar with the operation of the food trucks. How would she have known that Otto would offer Darlene food that day, though? She could have walked up to the table where the food was being collected and done something—but why?

That was murky, as was opportunity. And I knew I shouldn't be prejudiced because I had a record myself, but Keenwa's criminal history and her name change left her on my suspect list.

# Chapter 11
*Buttercup*

After I had found all I could about Keenwa, I discovered a website that listed the food trucks who regularly participated in rallies, and made a list of them in a separate column. I remembered meeting Otto Bergman, of Otto's Organics. He was the hipster, as Arielle had called him, who had organized the gift of food to Darlene Nowak, which put him next on my subject list.

The website wasn't very detailed—it only listed what each vendor chose to include. Otto, I learned, had studied at Johnson & Wales, where he had gotten his BA in culinary arts. I remembered that Arielle had said the hipsters were the ones with training, while the natives were those who cooked the cuisine of their cultures.

The gourmet burger truck only listed its owners, Mariana and Carmela, and I remembered one of them had yelled at Darlene Nowak.

I filled in the rest of the names, from Comida Peruana to Irie Master to the other guy Arielle had pointed out, Roly Ramirez, who owned El Rey de Los Pollos. It wasn't much, but at least I had something to work with when I went to the rally that night.

Then I put murder aside to think about suicide.

Besides the visit from Franklin Stone, I'd gotten a couple of different messages from members of the Integrated Response Committee, though they were, for the most part, academic blather about our responsibilities to our students. Nothing concrete.

When President Babson hired me to run Friar Lake, I had expressed concern about my abilities. I'd never managed a construction project or a conference center. "But you can learn, my boy." He clapped me on the back. "You have an Eastern College education. The ability to learn is what we teach you here."

Relying on that reminder, I plunged into learning about the reasons behind teen and college student suicide. The statistics were disturbing—suicide was the second-highest cause of death among young adults from 15-24, and the rate of suicide in that group had nearly tripled since the 1950s. Young men were four times more likely to die from their attempt than young women.

The first risk factor I decided to tackle was that suicides displayed a sense of isolation and lack of support. This was compounded by the presence of stressful life events, like moving away from home for the first time, and learning to live among strangers in an unfamiliar environment.

The easy way to attack that was to make sure that all our new student materials had a section on psychiatric help, with an emphasis on terms like "you are not alone." Could we include testimonials from students who had availed themselves of services and felt better? Colleges' promotional materials specialize in this kind of feel-good stuff, showing students of different ethnicities laughing together around bonfires.

I was over twenty years out of college, and I knew a lot had changed since then. I decided I needed someone younger to bounce my ideas off. As soon as I stood up, Rochester jumped up beside me, and he was delighted when I opened the door without hooking up his leash.

Friar Lake was empty that day, because we had no events planned, so it was easy to let him romp around from tree to tree.

Once he figured out I was heading to Joey's office, he half-followed, half-led the way.

The gray stone building that housed Joey's office had once been the cottage of the monastery healer, a small, square room lined with shelves. The campus architect had designed a long, low addition that sprawled off to the side, made of concrete block and covered with shiplap siding. Joey's office was in the original building, while all the tools and equipment that kept Friar Lake running were stored in the addition.

When I walked inside, I saw Joey sitting on the poured concrete floor with his hands in the guts of a lawnmower. "Getting ready for the spring?" I asked, as I walked over to him. That part of the building wasn't as well-insulated as the rest, and it was chilly.

"Yeah, I'm oiling up all the equipment. What's up?"

"Can I brainstorm with you while you work?" I asked. "I'm putting together ideas for this suicide committee and I need some younger perspective."

"I'm coming up on my tenth reunion next year. So I'm not exactly student age. But what can I help you with?"

I explained I was looking at the causes of student suicide and how to address them. "One of the big factors is kids who are away from home for the first time and have poor coping skills." I leaned against a workbench. "I keep reading about helicopter parents. What if kids who grow up with mom and dad on them about homework all the time don't know how to stand on their own, and that makes them fall behind, and get stressed?"

"You know my dad, so you know he was determined that my brothers and I were all going to college." Joey's father, Joe Senior, had recently retired as vice president in charge of the physical plant at Eastern. "And it had to be Eastern, because as an employee he got free tuition for us." He leaned back and wiped his greasy hands on a rag.

"It backfired on my brother Michael," Joey said. "It was like all his life he'd been focused on one thing, getting into Eastern, and once he started here he had no idea what he was supposed to do next. He fooled around, drank, skipped classes. You should have seen my dad blow up when Mike got put on academic probation his first semester."

"What happened?"

"Mike got his ass handed to him. If he flunked out of Eastern, then he'd have to pay for college somewhere else himself. Unfortunately for Mike he didn't get any of the handyman skills I got from my dad, so it wasn't like he could go do carpentry or plumbing or something. Suddenly he realized college was the start, not the end, and he shaped up."

He laughed. "I got reamed by my dad, too, for not looking out for Mike, who's two years younger than me. But Mike graduated with a degree in economics and went to work in software sales in Philadelphia."

"Were there a lot of drugs around when you were at Eastern?"

He shrugged. "Sure. Almost everybody smoked pot or at least tried it. Some of the richer kids had coke. No pills, though. Mostly alcohol. The biggest problem was in the frats, where guys were getting drunk every weekend and often getting in trouble." He held up his fingers. "You had impulsiveness, substance abuse and poor coping methods all in one."

I hadn't belonged to a fraternity while I was at Eastern. The ones I knew were either too rowdy or too rich. I didn't want to party every weekend, nor did I have the money to fly to the Caribbean for spring break, or drive to Philadelphia or New York to go clubbing. So I couldn't judge Joey's opinion, but I made a note of it.

As an adjunct professor, I was familiar with the academic alerts I was supposed to trigger when a student demonstrated a pattern of skipped classes or missed assignments. Advisors were notified to work with the student on developing better study skills and attendance habits. I'd used those alerts a couple of times, though I had never heard anything back from advising. I wondered if there was supposed to be a response system, and when I got back to my office I made a note to check about it.

I didn't get much time to think about the committee that afternoon, and at the end of the day I filed away my research and drove Rochester home, where I walked him and then drove to Pennsbury High with him and Lili for the food truck rally.

It was disorienting to return to the place where I had spent two very formative years, especially as the high school had been reorganized since my graduation. It had been divided into east and west campuses, and the one I'd attended was now called the East Campus. The building looked the same as I remembered – two-story windowless concrete front, with a big lawn and a flagpole on Hood Boulevard. I remembered occasional classes held out there when the weather was good, and hanging out there at lunch and after school with friends.

"This is where you went to high school?" Lili asked, as I pulled into the driveway that led to the parking lot. "It looks like a prison."

"Yeah, they weren't big on windows back then." The food trucks were backed around the sides of the parking lot, beside the bleachers of the football stadium where I had spent many Friday nights with my friends, cheering on the team, and where our graduation had been held.

I looked around. The sun was setting, casting a golden glow over the school and the ball fields, and the streetlights hadn't yet come on. Most of the trucks that had been at the shopping center the day before were there, including Otto's Organic and El Rey de los Pollos. Lili, Rochester and I went to Arielle's truck first, to say hello, but she was busy, so I left Lili to wait and walked over to Otto's truck with Rochester.

There was no one in line, and Otto was leaning out the front window of the truck. His muscular tattooed arms rested on the shelf, and he looked out toward the side.

"Hey, how's it going?" I asked him. "I'm Steve. Arielle's neighbor. We met Saturday at the shopping center in Stewart's Crossing."

"Yeah, hey." He kept looking around, then said, "Sorry, don't mean to be rude, but those cops are back again. The ones investigating Darlene's death."

I looked around and saw Jerry Vickers, but I decided to play dumb. "Really? Wasn't it just a heart attack or something?"

He shook his head. "They say it was murder. Poison. Arielle's their prime suspect."

"Can't be," I said. A truck rumbled past on Hood Boulevard and then its air brakes squealed.

"That's what I told them. Arielle's a sweetheart, and even though she was angry at Darlene, it was no more than most of us."

He stretched his arms out and it looked like he had a long phrase tattooed on the inside of his right arm, underneath something that looked like a big hat. It was vaguely familiar. "Can I ask you what your tattoo says?"

"Sure. 'You have great truths within you, if only anyone would bother to look.'"

That's when I recognized it. "That's the snake from *The Little Prince*, isn't it? I read that in French class in that building right over there."

"Yeah, I read it in French class, too, though not here, in New Hampshire where I'm from. It really made an impact on me."

Rochester was sniffing around the edge of the truck, probably scenting someone's dropped food. Otto's helper, Ramon, came up carrying a big tub of ice. "I'll put this in the cooler." He nodded his head to the left. "The cop is talking to Mariana and Carmela. Probably coming over here next."

"Thanks, Ramon." Otto shook his head. "I can't believe that any of us would hurt the woman. I mean, yeah, she was a bitch and she made a lot of trouble, but she was still a human being."

A cool breeze blew past, bringing with it the overwhelming smell of barbecue. "What kind of trouble?" I asked.

"You saw it Saturday. Always yelling at us, threatening to call the cops, calling them if she thought she had reason. If somebody's grease trap leaked in the parking lot, or she saw a rat."

"Were you the one who delivered the food to her?" I asked.

"I had everyone leave something on one of the tables, and I took the whole batch to her myself. And I swear I didn't do anything to the food. Why would I? All these people here, they're my family."

"Well, all except Darlene," I said.

"She reminded me of my great-aunt Hedwig," he said. "Her husband cheated on her, and after that she hated anybody with a penis. Even little boys like me and my brother." He shook his head. "Sad the way people get warped like that."

Darlene hadn't hated men when she was younger—but had the way either Jamie Quattrone or her ex-husband treated her changed her opinion? Did her overt dislike of the male gender make it more likely that a man had killed her?

A couple came up to order a veggie platter with quinoa, and I thanked Otto and headed back to Arielle's truck with Rochester, who was still obsessed with sniffing the ground. Arielle's regular assistant, Keenwa, was at the window serving up slices of quiche to a pair of teenaged girls. She was a skinny girl with coffee-colored skin and a huge pile of curly brown hair gathered at the top of her head and she looked cheerful and happy – not like a young woman with a bunch of dark secrets.

Arielle had stepped out of the truck and was talking with Lili by the side. "Can you take a quick break and introduce me to some of the other vendors?" I asked. "I want to get a sense of how everyone felt about Darlene."

She took a deep breath. "I can do that. I need to think about something besides the police."

Lili handed me the last of a ham and cheese croissant. The pastry was flaky, the butter between the layers nearly melting on my tongue. The ham was thin-sliced prosciutto, and the cheese was something nutty and rich like Comté. Arielle certainly used high-quality products.

Arielle and I set out, with Lili and Rochester. We stopped first at Roly's truck, El Rey de los Pollos. It was painted like a farmyard, with giant yellow chickens pecking at feed on the ground. In the background a white farmhouse stood next to a tall red silo. It was a cartoon image of what the farms around Stewart's Crossing had looked like when I was a kid.

Most of them had since been replaced by cookie-cutter suburban developments, but still, Roly's truck evoked a powerful sense of nostalgia. And the mouth-watering smell of the chickens roasting on a spit just inside the truck was a great motivator to step up and order.

Roly Ramirez was a bald guy in his mid-forties, wearing a white apron and a matching white bandanna. Arielle said something to him in Spanish, and Roly shook my hand. "Please to meet chew," he said, his accent thick.

Then he turned to Arielle and spoke to her in rapid Spanish. His words came out with a snarl, and I wasn't sure if that was his accent or his anger. She answered him quickly, then turned to us.

"I didn't realize you spoke Spanish, too," I said.

She shook her head. "Mine is very limited, from working with kitchen help in the past. Roly said he has to flip the chickens. He says to come back later and he will talk about Darlene."

"You don't have to speak Spanish to figure out that he didn't like Darlene," I said. "But coincidentally, Lili is fluent in that language." I looked at her. "Would you mind sticking around and talking to Roly when he has some free time? That way Arielle can keep introducing me."

Lili had never been comfortable with my snooping, either online or in person, and she'd often worried that it put me and Rochester in danger. Now I was asking her to take part in the investigation herself. I could almost see the emotions raging across her face. But I knew Lili, and I knew that if someone needed her help she'd step up.

Finally she said, "You know what Philip used to say to me when I didn't want to do something?"

Philip was her second husband, whom Lili had married while she was working as a fashion photographer in New York. I shook my head.

"Suck it up, buttercup," she said, and I could hear the bitterness in her voice. "So I'm going to do that. What do you want me to do? Ask him if he killed that woman?"

"Well, if he feels like confessing that would be a good thing. I was thinking more like asking him about his interactions with her. You don't need me to prompt you. You're a journalist. You know how to ask questions."

"A photojournalist. I know how to take pictures."

I raised my eyebrows and she relented. "Yes, I know how to ask people questions. But I've never investigated a murder before."

"And what is genocide if not murder?" I asked. "You were in Rwanda and Sarajevo." Then I thought of what those investigations must have cost her in emotional pain. I'd seen many of her photographs from war zones, and she had a unique ability to show her empathy for her subjects while portraying them realistically.

"But if you'd rather not, I can come back on my own and manage."

"I'll do it," she said. "Because one death matters as much to me as a hundred, or a thousand."

I leaned over and kissed her cheek. "And that's why I love you."

# Chapter 12
## *The King*

Arielle, Rochester and I walked on to the burger truck, which was painted with a background of a tropical beach—beige sand, bright blue water, and a fringe of brown and green palm trees around the edge. In the center of the beach was a grill filled with burgers. It was quite a welcome scene in the oncoming chill of the evening.

Mariana was a chunky woman with piercings in her ears, her nose and her eyebrows. I could see her in back at the grill, flipping burgers. Carmela, slim and blonde but similarly pierced, was up front. Arielle introduced me and Carmela said she'd be happy to talk if I came back when the truck wasn't busy.

I agreed. To the side of the counter was a tasting platter of burger bits, and I took one for me and one for Rochester. Mine was perfectly medium-rare, just the way I liked it, and accented with subtle spices. Rochester seemed to like his bit, too.

The next vendor we stopped at was Michael's Sandwich Yard. Like the other trucks, his was painted with a sweeping scene, in this case an outdoor café lined with tall oaks, where hipsters in man-buns shared beers and burgers beside a klatch of soccer moms in ponytails and yoga pants.

Michael was a beefy guy in his late thirties with tattoos up and down his arms, though his were curls and tribal symbols rather than the words in Otto's. "Michael's the sandwich king," Arielle said to me. "Any kind of sandwich you want, he can make."

She turned to him. "Steve's my neighbor. He's a sort of private detective and he's going to help figure out what happened to the book bitch."

It was weird to hear myself described as a "sort of private detective" when my only credentials seemed to be nosiness, a curious dog, and the ability to snoop around online. But Arielle knew how Rochester and I had worked with the police on the murder of the association manager, and she had made the leap.

"I only wish it had happened sooner," Michael said. "Bitch is too nice a word for that woman."

Arielle left to return to her truck, and Rochester settled on the ground. Michael's was the last truck in the line, and the crowds hadn't gotten there yet. "You want a sandwich?" Michael asked. "Challenge me. Anything."

"How about a Philly cheese steak?" I asked. "Sautéed mushrooms, no onions."

"You're on. I bake my own long rolls and slice my own beef." He leaned forward. "And I even use spray cheese for the authentic taste."

My mouth was watering as he began to cook. "She was trouble, Darlene?" I asked.

"You got it. And not just for us, for everybody. My wife's an author, you know. She self-publishes her romance novels because she makes the most money that way. But Darlene turned up her nose when Amanda asked to do a reading at the store."

"Funny, I heard she was nicer to women than to men."

"Yeah, well, not in my opinion. She told Amanda that if her books were any good she'd be able to get a 'real' publisher to put them out."

"And are they good?"

"Her first books weren't as good as the more recent ones, and she started hiring a proofreader, so that woman catches all the typos.

Today I say they'd stand up against anything from one of the big romance publishers. And she has hundreds of four and five-star reviews, too."

"Good for her."

"Amanda tried explaining the economics to Darlene— in addition to the proofreader, she hires her own editor and cover designer and layout person. Even with spending all that money out of pocket she makes a ton more because she keeps all the profit herself."

He shook his head. "Darlene was rooted in the old way of doing business. Which you could tell from how badly her store was doing."

The sizzle of the meat on the grill floated out to me, and I inhaled deeply. "She would have been out of business in six months, I bet," Michael continued. "One of the writers in Amanda's critique group was a friend of Darlene's and she said that Darlene's business was tanking, partly because she refused to move with the times."

He squirted the cheese onto the meat and after giving it a moment to melt, he scooped it all onto a fresh roll. "Anyway, good riddance to her. Sorry I didn't have anything to do with it myself. I hated the woman for the way she treated Amanda."

He handed me the sandwich and I paid him. I dosed the sandwich with ketchup and bit into it. "This is heaven on a bun," I said between mouthfuls.

"Tell your friends." A young couple came up, and Michael turned to them. Rochester and I settled at a table in front of Michael's truck, and I ate a couple of bites of my cheese steak. It was amazing, better than any I'd gotten in Philadelphia, even at the places that were supposedly the best.

It was so good it was gone almost immediately – though Rochester did help toward that. As we walked back to Arielle's truck to meet Lili, I spotted Jerry Vickers, in a navy sports coat and khaki slacks, heading toward us, and I tugged on Rochester's chain and slipped behind Roly's chicken truck, giving me a good view of the front of the burger counter.

"I'd like to ask you and your partner to provide blood and urine samples," he said to Mariana.

"What on earth for?"

"Just part of our investigation." Vickers handed Mariana a business card. "You can make an appointment with this lab. They won't charge you."

Mariana shook her head. "This is a violation of my privacy. I'm not doing it unless you give me a good reason."

Vickers pursed his lips. "All I can say is that an opioid substance was found during Mrs. Nowak's autopsy. Because the sandwich she ate was out in an area accessible to all the vendors, we're checking each one of you to see if you have the same substance in your blood or urine." He pulled a piece of paper from the inside pocket of his sports jacket and handed it to her.

"These are the relevant statutes. If you refuse to provide samples you can be charged with failing to provide a specimen as required by the police in the pursuit of a criminal case."

I tugged on Rochester's leash and we went around the back of the burger truck, then cut through the parking lot on a diagonal, back to the first of the food trucks. I wanted to put as much distance between me and Jerry Vickers as possible, because I didn't want him to overhear me asking questions and then perhaps complain to Rick.

The first in line was called *Gou nan Ayiti*. My parents would have been proud that my years of high school French enabled me to guess that meant "taste of Haiti" in Creole.

The man behind the counter couldn't have been more than twenty-five, though he had the happy grin and rounded body of someone who loved his food. A caricature of him beside the register said that his name was Leyonne, and he was surrounded by a pride of lions.

I didn't make the connection between the predators of the savannah and Haitian cuisine, but I figured it was a play on his name rather than a comment on his food. He was busy dishing up a fragrant orange soup for a couple who conversed with him in rapid

## Dog Willing

Creole. Then he turned to me and in flawless English asked, "Can I tempt you with anything, sir?"

"I'm just browsing now. But what kind of soup is that?"

"That is *soup joumou*. National dish of my people. Do you know that Haiti was the first black republic in the world?"

"I did not know that."

He scooped a dollop of the soup into a small cup and handed it to me with a plastic spoon. "This soup was reserved for the French overlords until independence. Now we make it on our national day, January first, to celebrate that we can eat anything we want."

The soup was rich and brothy, with shreds of beef and yellow squash, though a little too spicy for my bland American palate. "Were you at the shopping center Saturday?" I asked, as I took tiny sips.

"Yes, right near the front. But I had to leave early."

"I guess that's why I didn't see you. Did you know that a woman was killed there?"

"An awful woman. Worse than our French overlords, and that is saying a great deal."

"The woman who owned the bookstore?"

He nodded. "Do you know what she said to me once? That I had HBO."

I turned my head in confusion. "The cable channel?"

"That's what I thought. But she said no, I had Haitian Body Odor. HBO."

"That's awful."

"And I was born in North Miami," he said. "My father is a doctor and my mother a nurse. I guarantee you there was no body odor in my house."

"I can see why you didn't like her." I crumpled the paper cup and tossed it in the trash. "Thanks for the sample."

"Come back when you are ready for a full portion," he said, and then he greeted the next customer, a black woman, in Creole once again. She wore a business suit and high-heeled shoes, and I wondered idly at what made her nationality obvious to him. I figured it was the same unconscious radar that made me think someone I met was Jewish.

I had fed a good bit of my cheese steak to Rochester, so I was still hungry, and I circled back around to Arielle's truck and ordered a crêpe filled with chicken, spinach and Gruyère cheese. Even if she had poisoned Darlene Nowak I doubted she'd repeat the act with me when I was helping her.

I folded the crêpe into a V and bit into the end, enjoying the mix of crispy pastry and juicy chicken, when Lili returned. "Did you get anything out of Roly Poly Po-Low?"

"It's pronounced po-yo in Spanish," she said, rolling that double L in a way I knew I'd never be able to imitate.

She sat down on the plastic chair across from me. "He hated that woman, like almost everyone else. She complained about his accent and the smell of his chickens roasting. Though she used words like stink and stench."

"Well, she was a writer and a bookseller. Makes sense that she'd have a good vocabulary. Anything else?"

"She called the health department on the food trucks the last time they were at the center. Roly said he lost a lot of business because the inspector made him have his grease trap cleaned, and he had to leave early to take the truck in for service."

"But that's his fault, isn't it?" I asked. "He should be maintaining his truck."

"He told me he was a week away from his regular service, and there wouldn't have been a problem if Darlene hadn't called the inspector. The inspector told Roly that he had to solve the problem with Darlene or she was going to make all kinds of trouble, week after week."

"That's a motive. I wonder how the shopping center owner and the other tenants feel about the food trucks. Do they think they're a problem, or was it only Darlene making a fuss?"

Lili looked at me. "How do you do this, Steve? Think about this so dispassionately? A woman is dead."

"I didn't know her, but she was a human being, and she deserves whatever form of justice she can get. I try to put aside emotion and focus on facts. From what you've told me, Roly could be a suspect."

"He was angry about her, for sure, and he said that he was glad she was dead. But how do you figure out which one of these people hated her enough to kill her?"

"Rick always says that murder is about love, lust, lucre or loathing," I said. "The only men who loved her have long since moved on, so I think we can put love and lust on the back burner for now. I know her bookstore wasn't doing well financially, so without knowledge of her personal finances I'm going to focus on loathing."

I looked at her. "You've seen enough of the world to know that people will kill those they hate."

"But it's easier to understand when someone has lived under generations of hate for some other group. It's harder when it's so personal."

"I agree. It's difficult to accept that someone who looks like us, who lives in a civilized society, goes so far. A lot of people had strong negative emotions about Darlene, so the only thing I can do is ask questions and try to figure out who had the means, the motive and the opportunity."

I smiled at her. "I appreciate your help, sweetheart."

She laughed. "Was there a Hardy Girl?"

I shook my head. "Nancy Drew, though. Rochester will have to take Rick's place as the other Hardy Boy."

Hearing his name, he nuzzled my leg, and I scratched behind his ears. "Have any clues for me, boy?" I asked him. "Because I could use one."

He woofed, and then sprawled down on the pavement beside me. "He doesn't have anything for me now," I said to Lili. "But give him time. Roly may be the king of chickens, but Rochester is the king of dogs."

# Chapter 13
## *Painful Memories*

Lili's phone rang and she stepped ahead of Rochester and me to answer it, as we walked back to where we had parked. Rochester stopped to sniff a pile of typewritten pages that someone had tried to throw away, but just missed the trash can. I picked them up to complete the process when I noticed the heading "Food Truck Reverie."

The pages were clean, so I folded them over again and stuck them in my pocket. Probably someone's bad poetry, but I was interested in any information I could find about the trucks.

Rochester and I caught up as Lili spoke to her mother in Spanish, then ended the call with *"Te amo, mamita*. I'll call you tomorrow."

Once again I was impressed with Lili's ability to dart back and forth between languages, and the way her accent was perfect in each, even when she cited a Yiddish expression my great-aunts might have used.

We drove back home, and while the information was fresh in my mind, I tossed my jacket over a dining room chair and sat down at the table with my laptop to enter what Lili and I had learned into the spreadsheet. I added my impressions of the other vendors I had met, and what Lili had told me about Roly Ramirez and his run-in with Darlene Nowak.

By the time I finished, the spreadsheet still had big empty patches, but my plan was to return on Friday evening to the rally at Oxford Valley Mall and continue to collect information. I shut down the laptop and picked up my jacket to hang it in the downstairs closet. As I settled it on the hanger, I found the sheaf of papers I had tucked into my pocket.

I sat on the sofa with Rochester at my feet and began to read. It looked like the first five pages of a short story, which had been heavily marked up with a red pen. I thought the first line was pretty good. "A chill wind whipped through the orange and red leaves of the trees fringing the parking lot, swirling the smells of fresh pastry, rich stews and barbecued chicken wings."

Next to it, someone had written, "Elmore Leonard says never start a story with the weather."

Leonard was entitled to his opinion, I thought. But this sentence wasn't really about the weather, though it mentioned the chill wind. It seemed more like a descriptive introduction.

I continued to read through the story. Whoever had marked it up had hated nearly everything, though he or she had been careful to back up every statement with some piece of evidence or expert testimony, sometimes quite bitter. "Why should I care what this guy is wearing when I don't even know who he is?" was one of the more polite comments.

I'd never taught creative writing, but I had critiqued hundreds of college-level essays, and I had learned that you had to balance the amount of positive and negative messages you sent. I always tried to begin with a positive note, even if it was just "well-written" or "great introduction."

Then I focused on a couple of problems that the student had. I didn't want to overwhelm any writer with negativity; that's a quick way to get someone to give up. I was surprised at the amount of vitriol this teacher was able to squeeze into five pages. There wasn't a single positive comment, even though the grammar was correct and many of the descriptions vivid.

I remembered Michael Wilmot mentioning a critique group that Darlene ran. Was this from one of her students? If so, I understood why the writer had folded up the pages and tossed them.

From the material provided, I had the sense that the writer was someone involved with the food trucks. He or she was good at providing the behind-the-scenes information that readers often like. Though the teacher had balked at the description of emptying a grease trap, I found it interesting.

I put the pages aside. Maybe at the next food truck rally I'd be able to figure out who wrote them, and under what circumstances. When I went upstairs a short while later, Lili was sitting up in bed reading an article on my iPad. "What'cha reading?" I asked.

"Article about teaching methods in art classes. Nothing I don't already know."

"Is it the same as critiquing a paper? You point out the good parts, suggest ways to fix the bad parts?"

She shut the iPad down and put it on the bedside table. "In a way. Creative people are often more sensitive about their work than average students. The work is supposed to come from your heart as much as your brain, after all."

"But you do want to make positive comments, right?"

"Absolutely. And in both writing and photography you can separate the art from the craft. I can compliment a student on focus, framing, exposure and so on even if I think the work isn't very interesting, or if it's trying too hard to generate a surface response."

"Meaning?"

"A certain subset of students likes to photograph graveyards," she said. "They think that by taking pictures of tombstones they're making deep statements about mortality. But sometimes a tombstone is just a tombstone, you know? You have to dig deeper. For example, you've seen those photographs of military cemeteries, right? You either get a close up of the cross on someone's grave, or a long shot of rows of crosses extending to the horizon."

I nodded.

"There's nothing wrong with either shot. They're honest and simple and I can comment on all the technical aspects. But to get emotional depth you need something more. A shadow that slices the cross in half. Get down to the ground and aim your lens up at the cross so that it takes up the whole frame. That's the art. But of course you need the craft to carry off the artistic instinct."

She smiled. "Not to mention, that tombstone the person is photographing could be his or her grandfather, and there's a whole emotional connection that the photographer has that isn't coming through to the viewer. You have to be very careful not to shut down their emotional connection to their work, or they could get frustrated or depressed."

"It's like the work we're doing on this committee, too." I had a moment of revelation. "We should include a faculty member from art and creative writing, too. They may get early inclinations that a student is in emotional trouble based on the content of the student work."

"That's not to say everyone who photographs graveyards is suicidal," Lili cautioned. "Sometimes they're just morbid."

"I understand. But we have to make sure that our training reaches the creative faculty, and maybe adjust what we say to make the connection to them and their students."

The next morning, I checked Jackie Conrad's office hours online. Since I had to drive over to Eastern's campus to deliver some contracts to the bursar's office, I timed my visit so I could stop by her office and say hello.

I found her peering at a document from the middle of a pile of papers, with her reading glasses on.

"Got a minute?" I asked, as I knocked on the jamb of her door.

"Steve! Sure, come on in. I have to say I haven't had a chance to do much research for the committee because I've been up to my neck in midterms."

She handed me a page of short answers. "Look at number two."

The question was "What is a fibula?" and the answer was "A little lie."

I laughed. "This person isn't serious, is he?"

"You might not think so. But then look at number six." She took off her reading glasses and leaned back in her chair. Her blonde curls spilled around the collar of her white lab coat.

The question was about terminal illness, and the answer was, "When you get sick at an airport."

I laughed again. "Okay, then please tell me this is an outlier. Our students really aren't this dumb, are they?"

"When was the last time you taught a class?" Someone began drilling outside, and the walls of Jackie's office shook.

"Fall term. And yeah, I guess you're right. Some students just seem to suffer from CRS."

She looked puzzled.

"Can't remember shit."

We both laughed, and she grabbed a pen. "I've got to write that one down."

I leaned forward. "I'm starting to collect information about causes of student stress, and I thought I'd see if you have anything to add." I held up my fingers and ticked off, "New environment. Physical illness which might lead to opioid abuse. Feelings of isolation—and on the other hand, lots of opportunities to date, and then for romances to fall apart. Lack of support, lack of direction."

"I'd add test and assignment anxiety," Jackie said. "I notice that as an exam gets closer, students get more and more agitated. *Is this going to be on the test? How long does a short answer have to be? Do you grade on a curve?*" She shook her head. "They lose sight of the actual material and focus on the test as a marker of success or failure, rather than a snapshot of what they know at any given time."

"Is there any system for reporting students with problems like that?"

She shook her head. "Not that I know of. We have the early alert system which I use if a student misses the first exam or misses several classes. It's hard to quantify the problem, because some semesters students will be very vocal and ask lots of questions, and other times no one will say a word. I have a link on my syllabus to the science lab, but unless a student tells me he or she has been there I don't know."

It was another piece of the puzzle. I thanked Jackie and drove back to Friar Lake. When I got there, I went online and discovered that the science and math labs both offered test anxiety workshops. I added those to my list of resources. Then I had to turn to my real job, because I had a series of events coming up in the next couple of weeks and I wanted to make sure every detail was complete.

I shut down the office at five and drove back to River Bend. As I got close to the turn for Sarajevo Way and home, I saw the back of a black-and-white police car sticking out into River Bend Drive a couple of blocks ahead. Call me nosy, but I couldn't resist driving slowly past there to see what was going on. I was stunned to see a uniformed officer escorting Arielle to the car, then help her into the back seat. It wasn't until I turned at the next street to circle back to my own address that I saw Rick's truck parked outside Arielle's house.

Rochester must have scented Rick in the breeze blowing through the half-open window, because he scrambled to his feet on the front seat and peered outside. "This doesn't look good, boy," I said.

For the next half-hour or so I was edgy, expecting Rick to come by and tell me what was going on, but I realized he was probably busy getting Arielle booked at the police station. I hoped she had an attorney she could call.

I took Rochester out for a walk, and was surprised to see Emma at the dog park—without Arielle. The yellow lab raced over to us and then she and Rochester took off.

I looked around and didn't see Arielle, or either Brandon or

Sophia. Instead I spotted a tall, dark haired man in a business suit, handsome in a slick, Eurotrash way. He was on a phone call, but when he ended the call and pocketed the phone he called, "Emma! Emma!"

"It's OK," I said, as I walked over to him. "Emma and Rochester are friends." I stuck my hand out to him. "I'm Steve Levitan. Arielle and I often bring the dogs to play dates here."

He looked at me suspiciously, but he shook my hand. "Arielle mentioned you. Pierre Brodeur."

"Is Arielle all right?"

"The police came by the house this afternoon to arrest her, which is absolutely ridiculous. Anyone who knows my wife knows she wouldn't hurt a fly. And she'd certainly never poison someone's food. She cares about her cuisine way too much."

There was a lot to parse in Pierre's comments. First, he'd called Arielle his wife, so I assumed that meant their divorce hadn't gone through. I appreciated his defense of her, but something about how much she cared about her cuisine made it sound like cooking was more important to her than anything else.

Including, one assumed, her kids.

"One of my former partners practices criminal law, so she's looking after Arielle. I had to leave a meeting with a potential donor and rush over here to look after the kids. They don't want to admit it but they're very upset."

"I can imagine." There was something false about Pierre but I couldn't put my finger on it. If the kids were so upset, why were they back home while their father was making phone calls?

"They're finishing their homework and then we're going out to dinner. By then Arielle should be home." He turned toward the dogs. "Emma! Come!"

She ignored him, so I took over. "Rochester! Emma!"

They rushed forward, and with some difficulty Pierre hooked Emma's leash. "Send Arielle my best," I said, as Pierre turned to leave.

"I will." I watched as he strode toward the gate of the dog park, Emma unwillingly following him. I always thought dogs were the best indicator of a person, and Emma didn't seem happy with her dad.

I was still upset by the time Lili came home, and I told her what I'd seen. "Poor Arielle." She looked at me. "Do you think there's a chance she did it-- poisoned that woman?"

"She had the means and the opportunity, but I don't see a motive. Unless Rick found something that he hasn't told me."

Rick didn't call me that night, or the day after, Friday, either. I was still determined to go to the food truck rally Friday night, though.

During the day on Friday I tried to work on my suggestions for the integrated response committee, but it was hard to concentrate. I kept thinking about Arielle and her kids. What if they were home when the police came? That must have been terrible for her. And how hard it must have been for her to call Pierre and ask for his help. If she was fighting for custody with him, this would be bad ammunition for him.

I guess I was lucky back in California. The police picked me up at my office early in the morning, and my first phone call was to an attorney I had met at a Silicon Valley tech mixer. He didn't do criminal practice, but another lawyer in his office did. Once he established where I was and what I was charged with, he got busy.

Mary and I both had cell phones but we used them primarily for work purposes. If I needed to speak with her, I called the land line at her office and spoke to her secretary, who usually took a message. Mary was a high-powered executive by then and was often in meetings or conferences.

I left a message that I'd be home late that evening, hoping that the attorney would get me out on bail. I was lucky that the court wasn't busy, and I appeared before a magistrate after sitting in a holding cell for nearly eight hours. My attorney argued that I was a married homeowner who was a low flight risk, and I was able to put up the bail using a credit card.

## Dog Willing

By the time I got a cab from the jail to my office, got in my car and drove home, it was after eleven, and Mary was already asleep. I didn't get the chance to talk to her until breakfast the next morning. She was angry, justifiably, when I told her what I had done, but we didn't argue. I kept my head down, like a bad puppy, and accepted her excoriation.

Eventually, long after we broke up, she admitted to me that she felt bad about her role in my problems—while reminding me that they were *my* problems, after all.

By the time I had to report to prison, we had already agreed to divorce, and she handled the paperwork while I was inside. When I got out, my divorce attorney handed me a key to a storage locker where my belongings were, and the receipt for the yard where Mary had put my car.

During my year in prison, my father died, and it tore my heart out that I could not be with him during his final illness, or at his funeral. All I could think to do was redeem the BMW, load whatever I could into its back seat and capacious trunk, and drive home to Stewart's Crossing, where my father had left me his townhouse in his will.

Even though the circumstances were different, I had an idea of what Arielle was going through, and all the pain I had felt back then came flooding back. Lili went up to bed early with a headache, and after I took Rochester for his last walk, I couldn't do anything but sit on the floor of the living room with my head against Rochester's golden flanks and cry.

# Chapter 14
## *Sensitivity*

Friday morning, I resolved to do what I could to help Arielle. I stood up and went back to my spreadsheet. Instead of trying to fill in the names I didn't have, I worked with the ones I did. What connections could I find between the food truck folks and Darlene Nowak?

Over the years, I had gained access to a variety of protected databases, through logins and passwords I'd found in the dark web, the part of the internet that honest folks don't see. I had subscriptions to a couple of different programs that could run names for arrest records, mortgages in default, and so on.

Rick could probably get all the same information I could, but he didn't have my skills at combing through data, and he had a lot of other work on his plate. I knew that as long as I didn't break any laws, he'd be happy with whatever I could provide him.

I started feeding names in: Arielle Brodeur, Otto Bergman, Rolando Ramirez. While that was working, I searched for last names for Carmela and Mariana, the couple who ran the burger truck. It took a lot of digging but eventually at the Pennsylvania Department of Agriculture I found a permit for the truck in the names of Mariana Echeverria and Carmela Sanchez.

That site was a bonanza for me. I plugged in the names of the other trucks present at the Stewart's Crossing Shopping Center the day of Darlene Nowak's death, and got ownership names for Dailyn Torres of Comida Peruana, Glenmore Short-Walker of Irie Master, Michael Wilmot of Michael's Sandwich Yard, and Leyonne Dorleans, who had given him the sample of the Haitian squash soup.

I put them all in the software, and then started evaluating my results. Arielle had no criminal record, but I found her degree from the restaurant school at Walnut Hill College in a Philadelphia suburb. She still owed ten thousand dollars in student loans, and her payment record had been spotty. She and Pierre Brodeur were co-signers on a mortgage for the property in River Bend, and with a balance of over two hundred fifty grand. She also had a personal loan for twenty-five thousand dollars secured in part by the food truck.

Some quick searching online indicated that starting a food truck operation could cost anywhere from fifty to two hundred thousand dollars, depending on whether you bought your truck new or reconditioned an existing one, among other factors.

Her loan debt didn't tell me anything about her guilt or innocence in the death of Darlene Nowak, though.

Otto Bergman had taken his organic interest to great lengths, running a marijuana grow house in the country town of Upper Black Eddy, north of Leighville. He had been arrested for drug trafficking, which in Pennsylvania meant twenty-five pounds or more of marijuana. The mandatory minimum prison sentence for that offense was three years, accompanied by a $25,000 fine.

His case had been dismissed, however, and it wasn't clear why. Had he ratted out an accomplice?

Like Arielle, he owed student loans for his education, in his case at Johnson & Wales in Rhode Island. Where could a young guy like Otto get enough money to start a food truck, when he already owed over forty-five grand? The grow house was an obvious answer— perhaps he'd made enough money that he could buy his way out of his arrest, and still have enough left over to start the food truck.

I made a note to ask Rick what he could find out. If Otto was in financial trouble, then despite his friendly attitude he might have been pushed to commit more crimes.

Otto also had four misdemeanor arrests on his record, for crimes from public intoxication to vandalism to resisting arrest. All of them were before he turned twenty-five, and in the last five years he seemed to have turned his life around.

I'd been drunk in public a few times myself when I was younger, and I was lucky I hadn't been arrested. And like Arielle, nothing in his record indicated that he had any connection to Darlene Nowak or any propensity toward violence.

Joey came in then and wanted me to walk the property with him before we shut down for the weekend, as we usually did, so I saved the results of my searches and emailed them to myself.

"I hear they're cracking down on drugs on campus," Joey said, as we walked.

"I haven't seen anything in our email about that."

"I was talking to my counterpart over there this morning. The police swept in and arrested one of his men who had a couple of bags of marijuana on him. And he heard through the grapevine that they picked up a woman from the dining commons, too."

"I wonder if they're going after students, too, or just staff."

"You know Eastern. If we can sweep something under the rug, we will."

"I don't want to do that with this committee I'm on," I said. "If we can find a problem I want us to deal with it."

Joey chuckled. "Good luck with that."

We found a couple of small things he would have to handle the following week—a loose drainpipe outside the kitchen, some low-hanging tree branches that needed trimming, and a pair of crows building a nest behind the church. We agreed to let them continue, because they were out of sight. Rochester barked at a pair of squirrels who were engaged in a mating ritual, one chasing the other up and down tree trunks and across branches fresh with new buds.

After I said goodbye to Joey I kept thinking about what he'd said. Was our integrated response committee just another way to ignore a problem? Throw a committee at it, and by the time they come to a consensus, the problem will either have been forgotten or grown so large that it demanded real action.

I had only been with Eastern as a staffer for a few years, but already I'd seen initiatives come and go. One year the buzzword was learning communities—pairing classes together so that students in freshman comp were required to take an ethics class which met right afterwards, or one in political science or sociology. The teachers created assignments that relied on both disciplines.

The next year no one was talking about learning communities anymore. Instead we were focusing on "grit," a concept promoted by a University of Pennsylvania professor who had written a book by that name. Her research demonstrated that students who overcame obstacles and managed failure well were often more successful than those with high test scores or native talent.

Then we moved on to an initiative to better utilize our college's academic success center. In the English Department that year we were focused on pushing up the number of visits there and tutor meetings.

All of these programs worked while we focused on them, but failed as soon as we looked away. I hoped that the integrated response committee wouldn't suffer the same fate.

The unseasonably warm early spring continued as Rochester and I drove home. I saw a couple of daffodils peeking out from under a hedge along the River Road, and all around us birds fluttered, mated and built nests for their families to come.

What thousands of human couples did, all around us. In some cases, like Mary's and mine, our children never arrived and we split up. Then there were those like Arielle and Pierre, who began families but couldn't stay the course. I was sure that there were statistics about college success for students from broken homes, and wondered if my committee should include them, too. You could even go back to their early childhood—did their parents read to them? Did they encourage their kids in extra-curricular activities like museum visits, concerts and parks? That was far, far beyond our mandate, and it wasn't up to us to reinvent the wheel.

When I was growing up in Stewart's Crossing, our schools had a vibrant program in the arts. I sang in the chorus and took summer classes in ceramics. The school often organized trips for us to New York, where we heard the New York Philharmonic perform their Young People's Concerts. We went to Philadelphia for exhibits at the Franklin Institute through our science classes, and our social studies teacher took us to the Museum of the University of Pennsylvania to see the archaeological exhibits.

My parents were always willing and able to pay the small fees involved in those events. I remembered, though, kids who never went on those trips. Was that because their parents couldn't afford the occasional five or ten dollars for bus rental and admission or tickets? Or did they think the programs weren't worthwhile?

How did that lack of childhood cultural engagement affect kids by the time they got to college? I knew some kids from rural areas who drank in everything Eastern had to offer because they'd been starved of those activities as kids. And I knew other kids who'd had every advantage, and preferred to spend their college years drinking, smoking dope, and sleeping late.

I began to realize that our Integrated Response Committee might have bitten off more than we could chew. What did we really need to do? On the drive home that afternoon, I went back to Tyler Benjamin. He had fallen through the cracks because of his drug use and the despair that led him to suicide.

That had to be our focus. We'd be the little Dutch boy, plugging our finger into one specific hole in the dike.

I fed and walked Rochester, tugging him along because I was eager to get to the food truck festival that evening. Lili, Rochester and

I left as soon as the dog and I returned from our walk. As we followed the country roads that would lead us to the Oxford Valley Mall, now lined with suburban developments rather than farms, I reminisced.

"This was the place to hang out when I was a teenager," I said. "Back then there was an ice cream parlor where they gave you free sundaes on your birthday. I knew one of the waitresses so whenever my friends and I went we said it was someone's birthday."

Lili smiled. "Ah, the idylls of a suburban childhood. When I was a teenager my family was living in Chicago and I used to go down to the Loop, ride the trains and smoke with my friends." She smiled. "Even back then I had a camera with me all the time. I used to make my friends stop and wait while I took moody pictures of litter. Then I'd submit them for the high school literary magazines with captions like "our throwaway society.""

It was interesting to get a glimpse of what Lili had been like long before I met her. "Were you always interested in photography?"

"I was. My first camera was a Kodak Instamatic that my aunt and uncle gave me for my bat mitzvah. I had braces then, and I hated my curly hair, and I know it's a cliché but the camera gave me a place to hide, a protective layer between me and the rest of the world."

"Wow. I can't imagine you as anything but beautiful."

She elbowed me. "You are such a geek. Yes, my mother used to tell me that I was *una chica muy linda*, a very pretty girl, but I didn't believe her until the braces came off and my cousin showed me how to oil my hair to tame the wildness of the curls, and boys started to pay attention. Even then I was more interested in photography than dating."

She shrugged. "Maybe that's why I married Adriano when I was still in college. I had never dated much because I had that shield of the camera, and he was the first guy who not only valued my photography but also convinced me to put the camera down and live in the moment with him."

Oxford Valley Mall had changed a lot since I was a teen, with office towers on out-parcels, and the Sesame Street theme park nestled against one edge. As we were passing the park we saw a guy in a Big Bird suit holding his yellow feathered head and running awkwardly from one building to the next. Rochester barked.

We drove to the back of the mall, where the land was a bit higher and we could look out on the houses, stores and offices of the valley that led down eventually to the Delaware River. Dusk was beginning to fall, and the landscape was beautiful, streetlights beginning to wink on over the cul-de-sacs, store neons glittering, and above it all a blanket of clouds and a waning gibbous moon glowing an eerie white as it hung low on the horizon.

We didn't see Arielle's truck in the lineup so we parked at one end and started walking. One of the first people I recognized was Ramon, Otto Bergman's helper. I remembered Arielle saying that he looked like a movie star, but that evening he looked more tired than anything else. He hadn't shaved in a couple of days, losing the line of his soul patch, and his dark hair was tousled and greasy.

I hailed him and introduced myself again, as well as Lili and Rochester. "Are you a chef yourself?" I asked.

He shook his head. "I was trying to get a degree in medical records, but the school where I studied went out of business and I couldn't finish. I ended up with a pile of student loans and I can't go back to school until I get into a payment setup. So I'm going for plan B. I'm going to be a writer, instead."

Lili took Rochester's lead and continued forward while I talked to Ramon.

"Really?" I asked. "That's cool."

He nodded. "I've been working on my first book and it's very good. I'm going to self-publish it on Amazon and be the next Hugh Howey."

"I read *Wool*," I said. "Wasn't really my cup of tea but I could see why people liked it. Your book is science fiction, too?"

He shook his head. "Medical thriller. My hero is a guy who manages medical records for a doctor's office and discovers irregularities in the billing. He suspects the doctor is cheating Medicare and he assembles the proof, but then his life is threatened, and he has to go on the run."

"Sounds like it has a lot of potential."

"Michael Wilmot's wife Amanda is a writer, too, and he put me in touch with her and this critique group the bitch who owned the bookstore put together. Apparently she was some fancy writer once upon a time, though she never actually wrote a novel."

He wiped his arm across his forehead. "Darlene hated my first chapter and I kept obsessively looking at the way she marked up my pages, until I finally threw them away the other day. Sometimes you just have to push forward and write what you believe in."

I remembered the pages I'd picked up from the trash. They weren't bad, and if they were Ramon's I hoped he'd keep working on them. "Good luck with it," I said. "I'll look for it on Amazon when you get it finished."

"I've got to make this work, even though Darlene told me that a guy like Hugh Howey is one in a million lucky. My girlfriend and I have a little boy, and I need to do right by them. I want to marry her and be a good husband and father, but I have to get my own shit in order first."

He hurried off in the direction of the food trucks and I followed, thinking. I'd heard about students who had been scammed by those for-profit colleges but talking to Ramon made it more personal. How could the government let this kind of thing go on? This kind of trauma had to be adding to the rise in academic-related suicides. Not everybody was lucky enough, or smart enough, to go to a very good private college like Eastern, but the problems we were seeing had to be echoed at two-year colleges and public universities.

An idea began to take shape in my head, and when I reached Lili, standing outside the Comida Peruana truck, I shared it with her. "It seems like a lot of people connected to the food trucks went to Darlene Nowak's writing workshops," I said. "Arielle's daughter Sophia, Michael Wilmot's wife, and now I just heard about Otto's helper Ramon. He's got a lot at stake right now and I could see him getting angry if Darlene knocked down his dreams."

"Writers can be very sensitive about their work," Lili said. "Trust me, I've worked with enough reporters to know that they consider every word sacred. If Mrs. Nowak was rude to writers about their stories, I wouldn't be surprised if they got upset."

"It strikes me that there could be a whole group of other suspects beyond the food truck operators who had a motive to kill Darlene Nowak. Maybe the food truck rally was just a convenient location, and the real reason someone killed her is something very different."

"Sounds like a theory you should run past Rick," Lili said.

"I'm sure he's got his hands full. And right now it's just a hypothesis. I need some more data before I can suggest it to him."

We passed on the Peruvian cuisine, which looked suspiciously to me like the kind of mystery food we were fed in high school—a piece of protein surround by starches and covered in a pool of glop. Lili had been to Haiti and warned me the food at Leyonne's truck was too spicy for me, so we kept on going.

We stopped at the burger truck, where Rochester remembered the taste of burger I'd given him the other day. Either that or the smell of grilled meat put him into a swoon, and he looked up at me expectantly, with that kind of mournful, "Please, Dad" expression I could never resist.

I ordered a plain burger for him, and one with pork belly and swiss cheese for myself. Lili asked for hers adorned with sautéed mushrooms and onions.

While we waited, I saw Ramon dumping a bucket of ice behind Otto's truck, and I left Rochester with Lili and walked over to him. He might be an easy way to get into the critique group and see what they thought of Darlene Nowak, and why they'd met with her in the first place if she was so negative about their work.

"I've been thinking about writing a book myself," I said. "Do you think I could sit in on one of your critique group meetings to see how you guys do it?"

He shrugged. "If you want. Our next meeting is tomorrow afternoon at the Starbucks on US 1 in Levittown. One o'clock. If you give me your email address, I can send you my chapter."

"That would be great. I'd love to read it."

We swapped addresses, and then he had to returned to Otto's truck.

I felt a little better. At least I had a plan.

# Chapter 15
## *Instruments of Justice*

By the time I returned, Lili had retrieved the burgers and a platter of lightly spiced and salted French fries, as well as two sodas, and she had staked out a small round table for us. I slid into my seat and broke off a piece of burger for Rochester, nearly burning my fingers. I held it up by the edge and blew on it, while the big dog sat eagerly beside me, his nose up in the air and his mouth open.

I handed the bit to Rochester, who gobbled it up. Then I turned to Lili. "Ramon says that his critique group is meeting tomorrow afternoon. I asked if I could come sit in, and he said sure."

Lili picked up a French fry. "Are you thinking of writing a book?"

"He thinks I am."

"Then you ought to come up with an idea for one," Lili said. "What about a guy who solves crimes with his golden retriever?"

"I don't think anyone will believe that. I have a hard enough time convincing Rick, and he knows the real story of how Rochester has helped."

I thought while I bit into my burger. It was delicious, a great combination of medium-rare meat, tangy pork belly and smooth Swiss cheese. Some juice leaked out of my mouth and I had to wipe it with a napkin. Then I had to feed Rochester another piece of his burger and take another bite of mine.

Finally I said, "I heard enough stories when I was in prison that I ought to be able to find one I could fabricate a book about."

"Of course, everyone you were there with was innocent, right?"

I shook my head as I took a couple more fries. "Most of the guys I hung around with were white-collar criminals, and they knew they had screwed up. A bunch of them felt they'd been improperly prosecuted, or persecuted, to make a statement. But they were smart enough not to talk about their cases too much."

I fed another piece of burger to Rochester. "I might say I'm writing a book about what causes someone to commit those kind of crimes—embezzlement, tax evasion, that kind of thing. I'm still fascinated with a couple of those guys, who had tons of money, but it was never enough."

"You never cease to amaze me," Lili said.

We finished the burgers, fries and sodas, but before we left the truck area I told Lili I wanted to talk to Mariana at the window, while there was a temporary lull in customers. "You think you could come up and translate if I need?"

"*Por un centavo por una libra*," she said. "In for a penny, in for a pound."

"What would I do without you?" I leaned over and kissed her.

"Get into even more trouble than you already do," she said, but she stood up and led the way over to Mariana.

"*Que deliciosas hamburguesas*," Lili said, and Mariana replied in rapid Spanish. They talked for a couple of minutes, and then I heard "*mujer de la librería*," which I took to be "woman from the bookstore."

There was a lot more back and forth, and Rochester started to get impatient. I petted him and reminded him that he'd just had a burger.

Eventually a couple of customers came up and Lili said goodbye. Then she hooked her arm in mine as we walked away. "I know it's terrible to speak ill of the dead, but everything I hear about that woman makes her seem even more awful."

"What did Mariana have to say?"

"She's from Guatemala, and she came here legally with her parents and her brother and sister when she was a kid. She had an aunt here already who sponsored her family. But Carmela is from El Salvador, and she and her mother had to leave during the civil war there, when her father was killed."

"That's terrible," I said.

"Tell me about it. I was in San Salvador for a while taking pictures for a story for the *Times*." Lili had freelanced as a photojournalist for some of the nation's most impressive publications, including the *New York Times*, *The Washington Post*, and the *Wall Street Journal*. She shuddered. "Imagine if she was one of those little kids I photographed back then. How weird a coincidence that would be."

"At least she made it here."

Lili nodded, and we walked along in silence for a moment. Though there was no wind, a chill had risen, and even after the warm burger I was getting cold.

"Carmela was lucky, though. The DACA act came through six months before she turned eighteen, and she applied immediately for a renewable two-year exemption from deportation. Since then, she's been renewed three times, but she still can't become a citizen. She and Mariana married last year, and Carmela got a travel document so she could go back and apply at the embassy in San Salvador as a spouse of a citizen."

"Wow. It's incredibly lucky that both the Dreamer's Act and same sex marriage got approved. Without both of them Carmela would be out of luck."

"I know. If the act had passed six months later, Carmela wouldn't have been able to apply before her eighteenth birthday, and all the rules change after that."

"Are they going to be able to get citizenship for Carmela?"

"Mariana says everything should go through, but then she

laughed and said *haz changuitos*, which means make little monkeys but roughly translates to keeping fingers crossed."

"I heard you say something about the woman from the bookstore," I said.

"Oh, yeah. Apparently Darlene Nowak often criticized the food vendors for being illegals, and she was always threatening to call ICE on them. That made Mariana very nervous."

"I can imagine. I wonder, though, why people from the trucks went to Darlene's group when she was so negative about their business."

"Being an artist is such a solitary gig," Lili said. "I was lucky that I had a market for my photography, that I had editors who wanted to work with me, who discussed what I was doing and gave me critiques. It's hard to find that kind of feedback if you're not in school and you're not a professional. I think probably Darlene wasn't as nasty as people say, and that they were glad to get some kind of help from someone with a degree and some publication behind her."

We were almost at the car by then, and as I fumbled for my keys I dropped Rochester's leash. You'd think he'd have been full by then, or tired, but he took off back toward the food trucks.

"Oh, crap," I said. "Rochester!"

I beeped the car open. "Back with the hound," I said.

I rushed down the hill toward the trucks, behind Rochester's galloping form. I knew there was no use trying to stop him; he'd wait for me to catch up when he was ready. I saw him approach the pizza truck, the last one in the line, and then come to a sudden halt.

When I got there I found him sitting on his haunches, with a whole slice of pepperoni pizza dangling from his jaw. "Rochester!"

A woman was kneeling a few feet away, snapping pictures of him and the pizza.

"Don't blame him," the woman said from behind the counter. "That little boy over there, he dropped his slice." She nodded to a boy sitting at one of the plastic tables. "I just made the boy a new one."

I pulled out my wallet. "I should pay you for it."

She waved her hand. "We were going to have to put it in the trash but your dog scooped it up."

I glared at Rochester, but he sat down on all fours and took a huge chunk out of the pizza. I hooked his leash up and stood beside him. "I haven't seen your truck in a while," I said to the woman. "Not since the rally at the shopping center in Stewart's Crossing."

"Madre mia," the woman said, and crossed herself. "That poor woman."

"Did you know her?"

She shook her head. "We just start this truck a few weeks ago. That was our first time at that town."

"You didn't see anything then, did you?"

"No. Our truck was at the other end." A family came up to the counter, and by then Rochester was finished eating. I tugged on his leash, and he followed me back up the hill to the car.

"Rochester provide any new clues?" Lili asked.

"Not as far as I know," I said. I told her about the pizza incident as I slid into the car, with Rochester in the back seat. He licked his lips and settled down.

When we got home, I added the information about Ramon, Mariana and Carmela to the spreadsheet. For good measure, I threw in the pizza truck, even though the woman there had little connection to the crime.

Then I went back to what the programs had found for others.

Roly Ramirez had a line of health code violations that would stretch from Key West to Havana, which made me feel sick about eating chicken from his truck. I was surprised he could stay in business, though perhaps because the vendors jumped from location to location nothing had caught up with him.

He wasn't the only food vendor in trouble, though. Dailyn Torres, the sweet grandmother who ran the Taste of Peru truck, had served a year in state prison for illegally injecting chemicals into the rear ends of women who wanted bigger booties.

Glenmore Short-Walker of Irie Master was a legal immigrant,

though I assumed that Darlene Nowak had made nasty remarks about his citizenship, the way she had complained about Mariana and Carmela. But unless he was convicted of a crime it seemed that he was secure in the US and there was nothing Nowak could do to change that.

Leyonne Dorleans had come to the United States after the earthquake in Haiti in 2010 and was covered under the Temporary Protected Program for his country. I knew that she'd harassed him, with that bad joke about HBO, and I supposed he was a bit more vulnerable to deportation because of the program he was in the United States under.

But did these problems with Darlene Nowak give any of them a motive for murder?

The last name I had researched was Michael Wilmot of Mike's Marvelous Meats. He didn't fit under either of Arielle's categories as hipsters or natives; he didn't have culinary training, but he wasn't cooking a cuisine native to him either. He had been an accountant and amateur home chef until he entered a reality TV competition.

He hadn't won the competition, but he had won a burger challenge that awarded him $25,000 and the mentorship of one of the show's judges. He had used the money to buy and outfit his truck, and the famous chef supposedly came around periodically to check on him and offer advice.

According to the database, he had been married to his wife Amanda for ten years, and they had two young children and a hefty mortgage on a house in one of the massive developments between Stewart's Crossing and Levittown. No criminal record and he was in no danger of anything Darlene Nowak could do to him – other than say mean things about his wife and her writing talent. And if her income was important to their household, he wouldn't want Darlene discouraging her.

Lili called me upstairs a little later, and we binge-watched TV until Rochester's late walk, and our bedtime.

The next morning after breakfast and Rochester's morning walk,

## Dog Willing

I sat down at my laptop and roughed out an idea for a mystery novel about a white-collar criminal who has been falsely accused and has to work to clear his name. It was fun to put together ideas based on guys I had known in prison, and if pressed I could reveal my background and how I was using it.

Then I sat down to read the chapter that Ramon had sent me, which appeared to follow the chapter I'd picked up from the trash. The prose was really rough, lots of grammatical errors and misused words, but Ramon had a storyteller's gift to keep the plot moving and I was disappointed when I came to the end.

The chapter included comments from several of the other authors in the group. One woman, who was identified only as Miriam, pointed out all the grammar errors and included links to grammar sites explaining what Ramon was doing wrong.

Another commenter used the initials AW, and I assumed that meant Amanda Wilmot. She was very kind, noting all the things that Ramon was doing right. I agreed with her in general—she liked the way he kept the story moving, noting with approval the twists and turns he included in that chapter.

Rochester kept nuzzling me, though, so I couldn't concentrate on what I was reading. Eventually I sat on the floor with him, stroking his golden flanks as he grinned and salivated.

"Rochester," I said. "My romantic hero."

That reminded me of Amanda Wilmot, Michael's romance-writer wife. When Rochester rolled over and went to sleep, I got my laptop and looked up Amanda's books on Amazon. From the way Michael had described her career, I thought she'd be quite successful, but all of the rankings for her book sales were in the high six digits, and she didn't crack the top thousand in any of the smaller categories. I didn't understand what those rankings meant in terms of dollars, so I couldn't tell if Michael had been telling me the truth or not.

I clicked through and read some of her reviews. Though her first books got the occasional five-star one, most of them were threes and twos. Readers often complained about poor editing and formatting, pointing out errors like the change of a character's name halfway through the book, or the fact that the hero had dark hair in one chapter and was a blond in another. Several readers said this was a problem with self-published authors who thought they could skip all the steps that "real" publishers went through.

That was exactly what Darlene Nowak had complained about. If Amanda wasn't as successful as Michael indicated, then maybe Darlene's comments hit a sore spot with her—and with him.

The reviews of her later books improved, though, and it looked like Michael was telling the truth when he said she had begun to hire copy editors and proofreaders, and that readers had reacted more positively after that.

I was intrigued by the information I had on Ramon and Amanda, and I was looking forward to meeting them, the mysterious Miriam, and anyone else who attended that afternoon.

# Chapter 16
## *Critique Group*

Soon after that, I piled Rochester in the car for the drive to the Starbucks in Levittown. It was a warm day, and I saw Ramon and two women sitting at a table outside. I went up and re-introduced myself. "Glad you could join us," he said. "Get yourself a coffee and then you can meet everybody else."

He reached down and scratched beneath Rochester's chin, and my dog opened his mouth in a big grin. "I can watch your dog while you're inside."

"I can see he's made a new friend." I hurried in, got my coffee, and then joined the group, which had grown to three, plus me and Rochester. The first I was introduced to was Amanda Wilmot, who was younger than I'd expected, in her early thirties. Her blonde hair was pulled up into a messy topknot, and she wore a T-shirt and loose yoga pants.

Miriam Kagan was a heavy-set woman in her fifties with a silk scarf pulled over her head and knotted at the rear. She'd have reminded me of my grandmother except that instead of the housecoats my Nana wore, Miriam's blouse and slacks looked like they'd come from the kind of expensive store Mary had frequented.

The final member of the group was a sixty-something bald man introduced only as Fred, who had multi-focal glasses that made him look confused.

I'd only read what Ramon had sent me, so I sat quietly as the group went over Amanda's chapter. Ramon shared his copy with me, and she adhered to the lowest conventions of the genre, lots of heaving bosoms and erect members. Miriam was disdainful, pointing out all the clichéd language. But each time Amanda protested that Miriam just didn't know the constraints of the genre.

"Honestly, you're as bad as Darlene sometimes," Amanda said.

"Darlene, *olev ha-sholom*, may have been right occasionally," Miriam said, using the Hebrew words that blessed the departed.

Amanda crossed her arms over her chest. Fred said that he found the language very erotic, though he hastened to add that he didn't read in that genre. Ramon seemed to be the peacemaker. "I think there's a balancing act. Keeping to what your readers expect, but also looking for fresh ways to say the same things. You used 'heaving bosoms' in the last chapter, too, so maybe you could look for a different way to describe them in this chapter."

Amanda nodded grudgingly, and we moved on. Rochester had lodged himself half under my chair and half under Amanda's, so I figured he trusted her, and his opinion was important to me.

Miriam had written a chapter of her memoir about growing up in an Orthodox Jewish community in Milwaukee. Amanda showed me her copy and I glanced at it. It was lovely, lyrical writing, but nothing much happened. When Fred asked what the point of the chapter was, it was Miriam's turn to get defensive.

"There is no point," she said, emphasizing the word. "I'm describing my experience."

Rochester stood up. Whether it was her tone of voice, or whether he was bored, I couldn't tell. I rubbed my hand from the top of his head down the back of his neck a few times, and he settled.

"Even non-fiction has to make the reader want to continue reading," Fred said. He went into a long-winded speech about how he used fictional techniques like dialogue and cliff-hangers to keep readers involved in his magnum opus about the history of Pennsylvania from the time of the Lenni Lenape Indians to the latest wave of immigrants from Asia and Latin America.

Rochester didn't seem to have an opinion of Fred, or the chapter of his history of finding oil in Titusville that we discussed. I remembered a bit of it from school, and was pleased that I still knew the difference between anthracite and bituminous coal, but Fred's grammar was clean and his sentence structure varied, so I didn't have anything to add.

I zoned out and looked around. Each of the writers was prickly about his or her own work. But were Darlene's rude comments enough to make one of these writers want to kill her?

I popped back when we came to Ramon's chapter. I was curious to see what the other writers would say about it and had a few comments of my own. I found myself defending Ramon when Miriam complained about the detail regarding the financial scheme the hero had uncovered.

"I think Ramon has to include enough detail to make it believable," I said. "Right now, I think he's got a good balance."

"And who are you exactly?" Miriam asked, giving me a stink eye.

"I'm just a novice writer. But I've been reading all my life, I have a master's in English, and I teach periodically at the college where I work."

"Where is that?" she asked.

"Eastern College, in Leighville."

"Did you want to join our group?" Amanda asked.

I shook my head. "I just wanted to see what a group like this was like."

"Then you shouldn't make any comments," Miriam said.

"It's okay," Ramon said. "I'm open to any response."

I kept my mouth shut for the rest of the meeting, and I never had the chance to tell them about my idea for a book. Oh well, I wasn't going to write it anyway. I just wanted to have an excuse to sit in with them.

Ramon walked me out. "Thank you for defending me. The others don't understand the kind of book I'm writing."

"Why don't you find a different group then?"

He shrugged. "These are the only writers I know."

Rochester and I were in the car on our way back to River Bend when Rick called me. "You free for a brainstorming session?" he asked. "I know you've been talking to those food truck folks and I want to get your take on them."

"I just finished sitting through a critique group of writers who are marginally connected to the food group folks. So yeah, I have some ideas."

"I've been neglecting Rascal for a while, between work and spending time at Tamsen's. You want to come over here with Rochester and they can have a play date?"

I agreed, and I stopped at my house to pick up my laptop and my notes, and let Lili know where I was going to be.

"Why don't I call Tamsen and see if we can organize a dinner over at Rick's?" she suggested. "I haven't seen her in a while and I'd like to catch up."

I kissed her cheek. "That would be great."

I loved the fact that Tamsen and Lili not only got along but had become friends. I had noticed with Mary that if she didn't like one of my friends, eventually the friendship petered out. I think that was part of the reason why I had no one left, other than Tor Svenson, when I got out of prison.

I couldn't help thinking about the reasons for depression and suicide I had read about. One of the big ones was feeling alone, that no one cared.

I could have easily fallen into that trap myself. Tor was the only friend who kept in touch with me while I was in prison. I was lucky that the faith of those I'd met when I returned to Bucks County, Tor's friendship, and taking Rochester into my life had gone a long way toward pushing away those feelings.

I had been blessed, and I knew I needed to pay that forward, either with Arielle or the Integrated Response Committee, or both.

## Chapter 17
## *Chickens and Snakes*

Before I left for Rick's, I opened up Google and did some more searching, this time focused on the bookstore itself. I found a number of recent online complaints from authors who had put their books on consignment at the store. It did not appear that Darlene had left someone in control of her operation, which was still closed. There was a lot of frustration that there was no one to talk to about what was going to happen.

I made notes of each of the people who posted complaints, even though they had raised the problem after Darlene's death. Anybody could subscribe to the neighborhood groups I did, and it was not unreasonable that a small business owner like Darlene Nowak could do so. Suppose she'd used those forums to air her complaints about the food trucks? I knew she had been responsible for at least some of the health department complaints against Roly's truck. If he was the king of the chickens, she was the queen of the snakes.

Then I packed up the laptop, loaded Rochester in the car, and drove to Rick's, in the flat area between the Delaware River and the back side of Stewart's Crossing.

Rascal started barking as soon as I pulled up in front of Rick's house, and Rochester answered him. He didn't even wait for me to open the door on his side; as soon as I opened my door, he trampled over me and jumped out, rushing up to the gate to Rick's front yard, where he barked and whimpered until I got there and opened it for him.

By then Rick had opened his front door, and Rascal's black and white coat became a blur as the two dogs raced around together. They rushed past us, then circled around us like we were being herded. Rick picked up a rubber bone and tossed it, and the two of them took off after it.

We played with them for a few minutes, until Rascal raced inside and Rochester followed. From the front door I could hear them lapping at Rascal's water bowl.

"Thanks for coming over," Rick said. "I've been talking to all the food vendors and it seems like every single one hated the poor bookstore owner."

"I have a few more names to add to that. But let's sit down and go over the vendors and I'll tell you what I know."

When Rick's parents moved to Florida, he had bought their house from them, and he'd done little to change it. The appliances were avocado green, the floral wallpaper peeling, and the kitchen tiled with yellow and green squares. Rick brought out the last two of the Dogfish Head Flesh and Blood IPAs. We sat at the Formica-topped kitchen table, and I pulled up my spreadsheet on my laptop.

The dogs settle beside us on the floor as I said, "I'm sure you've already done your homework about arrest records. But just in case I found something you didn't know, here's what I've got on that."

I showed him the information about Otto Bergman's grow house, Keenwa Johnson and her boyfriend, and Dailyn Torres. "What exactly did she inject into these women's butts?" Rick asked.

"I didn't get that far. Probably fat, I guess."

Rick shook his head. "If Tamsen ever told me she wanted to get fat injected into her booty I'd think she was crazy."

"In any case, these three people have broken the law before."

"Allegedly, in the case of the guy with the grow house. Charges dismissed against him."

I took a draw from my beer, tasting the sweetness of the orange. "You're the cop. You must believe he was guilty or he'd never have been arrested."

"Innocent until proven guilty, my friend," Rick said. "Though privately I agree with you, and I'm sure he cut a deal. But poisoning a relative stranger is a big jump from growing some dope in your garage."

"I agree. Though he is the one who suggested the food donations, so that gives him both means and opportunity. He was trying to be a peacemaker, but he might have had deeper grudges against Darlene Nowak that we don't know about yet."

He took a draw from his beer. "That's three trucks. You have anything else?"

"Mrs. Nowak was very vocal in her anger against immigrants. She told Leyonne Dorleans, the Haitian guy, that he had HBO—Haitian Body Odor."

"I know I shouldn't laugh because that's prejudiced," Rick said. "But it is cleverer than just saying he smells."

I explained about Mariana and Carmela, their marriage, and their plan to get citizenship for Carmela. "If Darlene Nowak found out about that, she could have complained about Carmela, and that could have thrown a monkey wrench in their plans."

"It's only a motive IF she did something."

He pushed his chair back and walked over to a cupboard, where he pulled out a bag of blue corn chips and a jar of salsa.

"The threat alone ought to be a motive," I continued when he sat down again. "And she made a lot of health department complaints about Roly Ramirez, the king of the chickens, and she cost him business while he was shut down. Plus she made a lot of the same kind of negative comments to him, so he was resentful of her attitude."

He scooped up some salsa with a chip. "I spoke with him myself. He's not that fluent in English, but he makes his opinions pretty well known. He had a bad temper, too. He flew off the handle at one of his assistants, though I couldn't understand a thing he said."

"Yeah, when Lili spoke with him in Spanish, I couldn't understand anything except tone. But he struck me as somebody who'd get upset in the heat of the moment, not the kind of guy who'd plan out a way to kill somebody using someone else's food." I helped myself to a chip and some salsa. "Nor are you, I hope."

"You can be pretty comfortable eating anything here. Tamsen does a periodic run through my cabinets and throws out anything that's expired."

"Which reminds me. They're supposed to be bringing dinner over later."

"Then we'd better finish these beers."

As he picked his up, I went back to my suspect list. "Then there's Michael Wilmot. He has the same motives as Arielle, only he was also angry at the way Darlene was rude to his wife. She's a self-published romance writer and Darlene stuck up her nose and wouldn't let Amanda give a reading at her store. And if she kept making trouble for the food trucks he could lose business, like Roly Ramirez."

I picked up the list of writers in the critique group. "Amanda Wilmot is a member of this critique group that started at Nowak's bookstore, and then when Nowak became too toxic, the group moved out on their own."

I finished the last of my beer. I wanted another, but knew I ought to wait until we started dinner. "You said Mrs. Nowak was a published author, didn't you?" Rick asked. "Is that what gives her the authority to run this group?"

"She also had a graduate degree in creative writing from the Iowa Writer's Workshop, which is pretty impressive. And running a bookstore she must have read a lot and talked to publishers' representatives."

The dogs suddenly jumped up and rushed to the front door.

"That must be either Tamsen or Lili," I said. "We'll have to finish this later."

Tamsen and Lili, well aware of Rick's and my eating habits, had picked up a pizza and a big blue cheese salad from Giovanni's, in the shopping center in downtown Stewart's Crossing. Rick and I both liked the same kind—a thick crust with spicy Italian sausage crumbled and scattered over a base of homemade tomato sauce, freshly sautéed mushrooms and shredded mozzarella from an artisan cheese maker in New Hope. We'd converted Lili, Tamsen and Justin into believers, too.

Justin wasn't with us that evening; a friend's mom was taking him and a bunch of other kids to the movies and dinner to celebrate someone's birthday.

The four of us tabled the discussion of suspects in favor of dinner; however, we eventually circled around to Darlene Nowak's death. "I'm frightened by all the drugs they prescribe these days," Tamsen said. "When Justin broke his leg last year, the doctor wanted to give him oxycodone for the pain. I started to object, because I have heard so many stories about teens and adults who get dependent on these drugs. He assured me that if I controlled the pills and gave Justin exactly what he prescribed, he'd be fine."

"And was he?" Lili asked.

Tamsen nodded. "He was, but I was very careful and shifted him to ibuprofen as soon as the pain got more manageable."

"The ones who get addicted are usually older than Justin," Rick said. "They're old enough to control their own medications, for starters, and they may already have some experience of drinking or medicating to get high. They simply exaggerate the pain to the doctor, who keeps the prescriptions coming. Or the kid finds someplace that sells them. Kids can be very resourceful these days, especially with the internet at their fingertips."

I wiped my hands on my napkin. "With the right access, anybody can find opioids online, place an order and have them delivered to the house. Almost as easy as ordering a pizza."

After dinner Lili and Tamsen sat in the living room to chat, and Rick and I went back to my spreadsheet in the kitchen. I didn't have much to add about Miriam and Fred, the other members of the book group, but I found I was really intrigued by Ramon, his aborted education and the thriller he was writing based on medical records. "And I remember someone saying he was hurt in a car accident," I said. "Could he have been prescribed an opioid pain killer?"

"There's no way I can subpoena someone's medical records on a whim. But as you mentioned, it seems like anybody with an internet connection and a credit card can get hold of opioids these days."

After a while, we were just rehashing the same information, so we gave up and joined the women in the living room. When we got home, though, I decided to test our assumption. Could I find somewhere online to order opioids? How easy would it be?

The phrase "order opioids online" returned over eight million results. The first was an article from a UK publication about how easy it was to order such drugs and included the name of an online pharmacy that shipped within the UK. That company promised, "Our doctors will review and assess all orders to ensure all are safe and suitable for your use," but I knew, from a friend who had ordered banned weight-loss drugs from a similar site, that the review was cursory at best. And according to the article, as long as you randomized the credit card you used, the company did no tracking of how frequently you ordered a narcotic.

There were multiple articles describing how easy the process was, along with ads for online pharmacies, and only the occasional mention that buying such drugs might be illegal. According to one article, "Drug-filled packages with misleading labels have become a common sight at John F. Kennedy International Airport's (JFK) sprawling mail-sorting hangars, a front line in the battle against opioids. Many of the parcels originate in China, having been ordered on the web's darker corners."

The government was working to stem such orders and deliveries. Drug dogs sniffed the packages when they arrived, and federal agents posing as postal workers made "controlled deliveries" to catch distributors and end users. But just as with the attempt to outlaw alcohol under Prohibition, I had the feeling it was a losing battle.

Rochester was by my feet, chewing on one of his peanut butter bones, which I swear had to have some addictive qualities, because he worked them constantly, digging his long tongue into the bone to access the peanut butter in the middle.

The easy availability of these drugs opened a new angle in the death of Darlene Nowak. The killer didn't need to be an addict, or even an occasional user of opioids. Only some smarts and an imagination, and an awareness of the dangers of handling fentanyl.

# Chapter 18
## *Bullet-Proof*

Monday morning I picked up the Philadelphia *Inquirer* from the driveway, pleased that the carrier, who tossed papers out of his car at five in the morning, had managed to land it between Lili's car and mine. I glanced at the headlines, noted that the world was not about to end, and drove up to Friar Lake, Rochester beside me.

I answered the emails that had come in over the weekend, and then Joey called me and asked if I could meet him out at the largest classroom, where he needed to change the bulb in the overhead projector.

I positioned myself at the bottom of the ladder as he climbed. "You hear about the latest arrest on campus?" he asked, as he reached up high above his head to screw in the new bulb.

"More than the two you told me about last week?"

"I heard from a friend in campus security that this time they caught a student," Joey said. "He's got balls, I'll tell you. Ordered pills from China, and been dealing out of his dorm room."

"Whoa. You've got to be pretty dumb to do that—or have a pretty low opinion of our security."

"Or both," Joey said, as he finished with the bulb and motioned me to turn on the projector. While it warmed up, he stepped down from the ladder. "Or the third option. He's a teenager, and he thinks he's bullet-proof."

The projector came on, and I walked back to my office with Rochester. I wondered where I could look for information about the student who'd been caught dealing drugs. Because I'd stepped away from my computer for a while, some automated software download program had kicked in. While I sat there and stared at the twirling hourglass, Rochester settled on the floor.

I heard him chewing on something and assumed it was one of his bones—but then I remembered one of my father's favorite sayings. When you assume, you make an ass of you and me.

I found it mildly titillating when I was a kid, because I wasn't allowed to use adult words like ass. I had to say that my behind hurt or that so and so had been kicked in the butt. And I certainly couldn't use "ass" to refer to a human being.

I looked down at Rochester, and he had the *Inquirer* in his paws and he was worrying the second section. "Are you trying to tell me I should read the paper instead of just sitting here staring at the computer?" I asked, as I pried the paper from his paws.

He had been nibbling on the upper right corner, and just below that, on the front page of the second section, was an article titled "Student at Elite College Caught with Drugs."

The photo immediately to the right of the text was one I knew well, a stock photo of Fields Hall in all its Victorian glory. I imagined someone from the college's public relations department meeting with President Babson right then, explaining, "At least they called us an elite college!"

The report was a textbook example of how to write a newspaper article. The first paragraph was a single line. "Earl Van Pool, 21, a student at Eastern College, was arrested on Saturday for possession with intent to deliver fentanyl, a synthetic opioid illegal in the Commonwealth."

The five journalistic questions – who, what, when, where and why all answered in a single elegant sentence. Perfectly readable by the average newspaper reader, who statistics showed had only a ninth-grade reading level.

The mug shot beneath it was not flattering—but then, mug shots rarely are. Van Pool had shaggy blond dreadlocks, glassy eyes, and a scruffy beard.

The article continued in similar style. "Van Pool, a native of North Philadelphia, resides in the Birthday House dormitory on the college campus in Leighville.

"He was apprehended in his dorm room after an anonymous report. Officers found three hundred grams of fentanyl, as well as razor blades and other drug paraphernalia. Shipping labels indicated the fentanyl had been delivered from China to an off-campus mail center."

I had lived in Birthday House myself, and I remembered it as a rollicking place full of teenaged hormones mixed with students who were too smart to realize how little they really knew.

The reporter had interviewed Van Pool's mother, Aspecia Jenkins, who blamed his problems on the year he spent at Liberty Bell University where he had studied to be a pharmacy tech. "Too many drugs there," she complained. "I didn't want him getting mixed up in no drugs. He too smart for that."

I knew all about Liberty Bell. It was one of the for-profit degree factories that had sprung up like toxic mushrooms. Earl Van Pool had gotten out just in time—the school had been accused of financial aid fraud the previous summer and shut down a few weeks before Christmas.

I had some small part in that shutdown. I had been investigating the death of a high school friend's husband, which had led to the discovery of a scam he'd been part of at Liberty Bell. The fallout from his death had in part led to the school's closure.

The article concluded that Van Pool was being held in the Bucks County Jail in Doylestown. He claimed that his father was a Dutch student who had impregnated his mother during a junior year at the University of Pennsylvania, and that therefore he had dual citizenship and wished to be extradited to the Netherlands, where he believed drug dealing was not against the law.

My computer had finished booting by then, and I opened my email program to find a new message from Jackie Conrad about the progress of the Integrated Response Committee. "The president wants to know when we are meeting next, and how soon we will have recommendations. Can we schedule another meeting for Tuesday afternoon?"

I accepted the meeting request, and then emailed Jackie that I had been doing some research into student suicides, and that I'd bring that with me.

Most of what I had found was directed at family and friends, rather than college faculty and staff. I prepared a handout using material from various sources, including eleven signs of distress, from agitation to depression, confusion to strange behavior. All of them, sadly, could apply to a varying subset of students on any given day.

I had been teaching at Eastern, on and off, for five years by then. I could cite examples of very needy students, who asked a dozen questions during and after class. Even more of students who came to class late, dozed through lectures, or otherwise let me know they didn't care about what we did together—as long as they got the grades their parents demanded of them.

Had any of them been at risk of suicide? I couldn't say. As far as I knew, no one I taught had committed suicide, at least not while they were still in school.

But had those typical student behaviors been symptoms of something deeper? On occasion a student had confided in me. A boy's mother was going through chemotherapy and he'd been too upset to work on his paper. A girl's brother had been killed in a car accident. Another boy had mononucleosis and the resulting fever and fatigue had interfered with his ability to complete assignments.

I had worked with all of them, and others, to help them overcome their problems and complete the course work, even if it meant submitting papers late. I didn't want to be the cause of someone dropping out of college, so I bent over backwards to make sure that didn't happen, though I did fail students occasionally, usually when they didn't come to class or do the work.

I wasn't sure how detailed to get, so I checked Jackie's class schedule and then called her office. After we said hello, I explained where I was in my thinking. "In most cases, we don't know our students well enough to make judgments on things like changing friends or spending more time alone than usual."

"Our standard science class enrollment is fifty students, and twenty-five in a lab that accompanies a class like anatomy and physiology. I usually teach two labs along with my three classes. In any given semester I might have two hundred students. I'm lucky if I get to know the outliers—the ones who are really excellent, and the ones who struggle."

"If a student doesn't fall into one of those two categories, it means the most we know about them is their names, and if we check the roster, their major."

"I make them put name cards in front of them so I can call on them by name, but I know a lot of professors don't like to do that."

"Yeah, I don't like that," I said. "If I'm adjuncting one term, and I have only twenty-five students, I feel like I ought to get to know their names based on their work and their personalities. It doesn't always happen, though."

I looked down at the list I had in front of me. "Some students just have bad habits when it comes to cleanliness, so not bathing regularly or brushing their teeth could be their normal behavior."

Jackie laughed, and Rochester got up from the floor and came over to rest his head on my knee.

I added, "However, a student who is normally upbeat and becomes tired or sad, or a good student who loses interest in doing homework—those are things we could take note of, if we're paying attention."

"I had a student last semester who spoke so fast I could barely understand her. I mentioned it to my department chair, and she told me to notify the dean of students, because that could be evidence of drug use."

"What happened?" I scratched behind Rochester's ears, and he opened his mouth in a big doggy grin.

"I never heard back. The student passed the class, at least. But the dean is supposed to contact the student, have one of those heart-to-heart talks about what's going on, and then if necessary give him or her referrals."

"I would like to know what happens when we put in one of those alerts." I picked up a pen and made a note on the pad beside my computer.

"I can ask my department chair if she knows," Jackie said.

"I can do that, too. I happen to live with a department chair."

"Send Lili my regards, and I'll see you tomorrow."

I hung up, and then called Lili on my cell phone, so that Rochester and I could go outside while I talked. I opened the front door and he raced out ahead of me as a voice I didn't recognize answered, with a tentative "Doctor Weinstock's office?"

"Hi, this is Steve Levitan from Friar Lake. Is she in?"

"Friar Tuck?"

I had to hold back my laughter. "No, the Friar Lake Conference Center at Eastern. She knows me."

I knew Lili's secretary, Matilda, so I didn't usually have to introduce myself as more than Steve. I wasn't going to introduce myself as her boyfriend, or significant other, or any other euphemism.

"Please hold."

Instead of getting the college's standard hold music, I heard a dial tone. "Rochester. Leave that squirrel alone."

He ignored me as I called back. "Hi, it's me again. Steve from Friar Lake."

I heard the young woman say, "How do I put a call on hold?"

From somewhere in the distance, I heard Lili explain, and then the hold music. A moment later Lili said, "This is Dr. Weinstock."

"Not a good day in the office, I guess."

"Matilda is out to lunch and our work-study student is manning the phones. She's a very talented painter."

"But her office skills are lacking."

"We all have areas we need to work on. What's up?"

I asked her about what happened when a student was reported for problems. "I can't say for sure," she said. "I know someone from the Dean's office reaches out, and there used to be a plagiarism video they had to watch, if that was their problem."

"But what if you think a student is having emotional or behavioral problems?"

"Then I'd speak to the student personally. You're not teaching this term, though. Has a student approached you?"

"This is for my committee."

I explained what I was putting together and Lili said she was sorry she couldn't help, but would love to know what I found out. "The fine arts tend to draw in students with emotional issues, and sometimes we have to focus too much on the therapeutic effects of what we're doing rather than the technical or the artistic."

"Speaking of artsy stuff, can we go to the food truck rally again tonight? There's one at an office park off I-95. I want to ask some more questions."

"You're going to make me fat, *mi amor*. But I will go with you."

"You will always be perfect in my eyes."

She laughed. "Smooth talker. See you at home."

I prepared a handout for the committee, but then decided the information might be more effective as a PowerPoint, broken up into separate slides. I worked on that for the rest of the day, fiddling with animations and adding graphics and statistics. Even though I was only a part-time professor, I wanted to show my colleagues what I could do.

Would what we put together be enough to help the students who needed it, though? Even the ones who thought they were bulletproof?

# Chapter 19
## *Everyone is Stressed*

I realized as Lili, Rochester and I pulled into the lot of the big office park between Yardley and Levittown that I'd been there before. Hunter Thirkell, an attorney I had known since I moved back to Stewart's Crossing, had his office there, in a co-working space in one of the new-looking two-story buildings meant to evoke the barns in the area, with big windows, a peaked roof and red shiplap siding.

We parked at one end of the lot and began walking toward the trucks. As we did, I noticed Hunter's distinctive bulk ahead of us. "Hey, Hunter!" I called ahead to him, and he stopped to wait for us.

Rochester tugged on my leash. In the past when we'd gone to his office together, the attorney had been a reliable source of treats for my always hungry golden, so it's not surprising that Rochester wanted to see him.

I flailed along behind the dog, who was pulling like he was in a sled race. "Still well-trained, I see," Hunter said, as he leaned down to scratch behind Rochester's ears. "Sorry I don't have anything to offer you. I was just going to walk over and see if there's anything worth eating from these trucks."

Lili stuck her hand out to Hunter. "You can walk with us then.

I'm Lili. We haven't met, but you must be Hunter Thirkell. Steve has spoken a lot about you."

"All bad, I'm sure." Hunter had a fat man's twinkle in his eyes, and I was sure he'd make a great Santa at Christmas – though he'd probably treat each kid as a potential client and discuss the contractual obligations involved in "being good."

We talked as we walked toward the trucks, giving Hunter our recommendations. He liked his food spicier than we did, so Lili suggested the Haitian truck. "Try the soup and see if you like it."

"I will. What are you up to these days, Steve? You aren't here because of that murder at the food truck rally a week and a half ago, are you?"

"You know me too well. We were there that day, and I was the one who found the body."

"Not Rochester?"

"Not this time. The woman who's been accused lives in River Bend, and Rochester and her dog Emma are friends."

"Ergo, you're involved," Hunter said. "You know, any time you want to set up a shingle as a private investigator, I'll start sending work your way."

"Maybe after I retire from Eastern."

We reached the first truck, Gou Nan Ayiti, and left Hunter examining the Haitian menu. At Arielle's Cuisine de France, despite the delicious aromas of butter and chocolate emanating from the truck, there was no line, as there was at many of the other trucks. I wondered if people had read about her in the news and were staying away from her food out of fear.

Keenwa called Arielle out from the back, and she met us at a table in front of the truck. Arielle had dark circles under her eyes, and her white blouse hung loosely from her shoulders, as if she'd been losing weight. "How are you holding up?" I asked

"I'm so stressed I can't eat. The police won't leave me alone—that Detective Vickers calls me again and again with little questions. I keep losing things and forgetting things. This morning I even forgot to make lunches for the kids, which I always do."

"That's understandable given the stress you're under." Lili reached out and squeezed Arielle's hand. "Steve is looking into things and I'm sure he'll figure out what's going on soon."

I wished I had Lili's confidence.

"It's not just me, it's Keenwa too. She says the police are harassing her, and every time I call her she's asleep. I think that she's stopped going to her classes."

Those weren't good signs, from what I'd been reading. Did that mean Keenwa was guilty of something?'

"And my kids are holding up, but I know all this stress is having an impact on them," Arielle continued.

"Have you noticed anything about the other food truck people?" I asked.

"Everybody is stressed. You should talk to Otto. He's the one who put together the food for Darlene Nowak, and I think he's hiding something."

A young couple came up to the window and Arielle left us to go back inside. We walked over to Otto's Organics, where we caught Otto yelling at Ramon. "You've got to bathe, dude. We're serving food here. I can't have you coming to work smelling like a sewer."

"I've been working on my book," Ramon protested. "Sometimes I get so caught up in it I forget to do stuff."

"Well, don't come to work tomorrow unless you've taken a shower."

Poor hygiene was another symptom of drug abuse. Was I going to start seeing those signs everywhere?

Otto turned and realized we were standing there. "Just a little employee guidance," he said. "What can I get for you?"

We hadn't tried Otto's food yet, so Lili ordered a plate of sautéed brussels sprouts with chicken, and I splurged on the lobster mac and cheese, over a platter of pasta.

Otto talked while he cooked. In rapid fire, he told us the cheese was sourced from a farm where the cows grazed on pesticide-free grass. The pasta was made with durum wheat grown in a similar environment. "Got to respect our mother," he said, as he stirred the brussels sprouts in olive oil, then dosed the pan generously with chardonnay. "You get two mothers in this life. Your birth mom and then mother earth. Both of them need love."

I couldn't argue with that. Like the student I'd had in the past, Otto jumped quickly from topic to topic, sometimes throwing out non-sequiturs. In the background I saw Ramon moving around slowly, and he seemed tired and sad—the opposite of what I expected if he'd been busy writing.

Ramon stepped out the back of the truck, and while Lili paid Otto for the food I stepped around to catch him. It felt weirdly isolated back there, shielded from the crowd by the bulk of the trucks. "I really enjoyed the chapter you submitted to the group," I said. "Do you have any more written I could look at?"

"I have the first three chapters. I can email them to you."

"I'd like that. You have a good way with plot."

"It's all based on what happened at the doctor's office where I worked. I'm running into problems now because things are happening that are different, and I'm not sure how I can rope them all together."

That didn't sound like what he had told Otto, that he'd been so caught up in his work that he forgot to shower. But maybe it was all part of his creative process.

I sat with Lili to eat, and our food was wonderful. We shared the rich lobster mac and cheese and the savory brussels sprouts, coated with bread crumbs and bacon bits, and then complimented Otto profusely. "Tell your friends," he said, and then he had to turn to the next customer.

Since there was no line at Michael's Sandwich Yard, I stopped to tell Michael that I had met his wife that weekend and really enjoyed reading her chapter. It was only a white lie, and I thought it might get him to open up.

"I keep telling her to dump that group," he said. "They're holding her back, always giving her things to change. Right now she needs to focus on getting more books out." He shook his head. "I swear, though, as soon as she puts one out somebody is pirating it and giving it away free. I spend half my time looking at all these pirate sites."

"You need to be careful of those," I said. "Make sure they're not attaching spyware to anything you download."

"Oh, I'm careful. I only use the Tor browser and open incognito windows in Chrome so that no one knows who I am."

It had been my experience that people who bragged about their security online didn't know what they were talking about, but Michael seemed more knowledgeable than most. It was interesting that he knew about the dark web, and I wondered if he'd ever stumbled on a site selling fentanyl.

We ran into Hunter again. He had loved the Haitian stewed chicken, and we recommended he stop at Arielle's for dessert.

That reminded me of the article I had seen about Earl Van Pool, and his arrest for possession of fentanyl. I asked Hunter if he'd seen it, and he had.

"Do you think he can be extradited to the Netherlands?" I asked.

Hunter laughed. "In the first place, it's not like he has diplomatic immunity or anything. I read another article in which his mother said she never married the father, or registered the kid for dual citizenship."

We started walking back toward Arielle's. "I had a case a year or two ago, a Dutch woman who was arrested with a couple hundred fake Restoril tablets in her luggage. Restoril is a benzodiazepine, and it's a controlled substance here. It's also on List 1 of the Opium Law in the Netherlands, along with fentanyl and a hundred and fifty other drugs."

"What happened?" I asked.

"I arranged a plea deal and she fingered the guy who asked her to transport the drugs. She went back to Amsterdam to serve her time. But I don't think that will happen with this kid."

Even though Van Pool's argument was based on a faulty premise, it showed that he was smarter than the average drug dealer, and intellectually capable of transferring to Eastern, where he had nearly completed his sophomore year

While I ushered Hunter over to Arielle's truck and introduced him, Lili spoke briefly to Roly the chicken king.

When we met up at the car, she told me Roly was worried about the next visit from the state food inspector. "He's afraid Darlene did something to screw him over before she died. More reports or complaints. '*Estoy on ascuas*,' he said, which is like being on pins and needles."

"If he's keeping clean he has nothing to worry about," I said.

Lili glared at me. "He says the inspectors are all Anglos and they look down on anybody who has brown or black skin. They think because he speaks with an accent he can't possibly be able to follow all the rules."

Because Lili, like me, was the descendant of Eastern European Jews, it was easy to forget that she considered herself a Latina because she was the second generation of her family to be born in Cuba. "That's terrible," I said, because it was, and I wanted Lili to know I was behind her.

"I volunteered to come over the next time he has an inspection and help him," she said. "You're not the only one who wants to help people in trouble."

"I've known that about you ever since we met." It was true; in her photojournalism work she showed a passion for helping the disenfranchised, and I saw her caring every time we talked about a student in trouble.

I leaned over and kissed her cheek. "Just one of the many, many things I love about you."

At home that evening, our bellies full, I added more details to my spreadsheet. It was interesting how many of the vendors were showing signs of opioid addiction—sleeplessness, irritation, rapid speech, lack of focus. That also could have been because of the stress they were under while the police were investigating Darlene Nowak's death. They worked hard, for low wages, and struggled against a complex bureaucracy, sometimes impeded by language skills or citizenship status.

But these could be symptoms of someone who had access to the kind of fentanyl that had been used to kill the book bitch.

# Chapter 20
## *The Long Game*

As soon as I got to Friar Lake on Tuesday morning, I called Tony Rinaldi, the detective with the Leighville police I had worked with in the past when there had been incidents on college property.

"I'm working on a committee here at Eastern to …" I began, after I'd said hello. "I'm not sure how to describe it except that we're looking at the suicide we had last November, and at ways we can prevent more like it."

"What can I do for you?"

"I was hoping to talk to you about drugs on campus and in Leighville."

"The arrest we made over the weekend."

"Yeah, that prompted it. But I want to get a better sense of how big the problem is that we're trying to tackle."

"I'm pretty busy with the paperwork and the interviews for this case, but I have to eat. You want to meet for lunch?"

I agreed. Tony and I weren't as close as I was to Rick, but we'd become friendly over the years. I'd met his wife, who was a nurse at Eastern, and Lili and I had gone out with them a couple of times.

I spent the next hour or so on paperwork, then left Rochester with Joey at his office. I leaned into the stiff wind, which rattled the branches of the budding maples and oaks and turned the triangular pines nearly sideways.

The wind felt good, as if it was going to wipe away all the dark matter of the last couple of weeks and open us up to a fresh new spring.

I'd arranged to meet Tony at The Hungry Horse, a venerable institution that had been in business long before I was a student. It was a long, single-story building with a low roof that jutted out over the sidewalk along Main Street. Through the grimy windows I saw rows of rickety tables and booths with peeling leatherette. At least the food was good.

Tony was a chunky guy of about my age with a baby face and a head of thick black hair. We settled in a booth by the window and talked about his wife and his young son, and ordered our lunches. A BLT for me, the chef's salad for him. "Tanya's got me on a strict diet," he said. "She says I owe it to Frankie to be around and in good health for his college graduation."

"And he's what, three years old now?"

"Three and a half. Tanya's got her eye on the long game."

I lifted my glass of water and took a sip. "What can you tell me about drugs on Eastern's campus?"

"First of all, the problem isn't just drugs. Alcohol is still the most popular illicit substance on any college campus. Statistics show that over one third of college students partake of alcohol on at least an occasional basis. Even though probably ninety percent of them are below the legal age."

He sipped his water. "Eastern has done a good job of policing fraternity parties, but they're never going to catch everyone. After liquor, there's an ongoing problem with stimulants like Adderall and Ritalin. Kids use them to juice up for studying and exams. They say the drugs help them focus. That they get improved attention span and better concentration."

"That sounds like a good thing. Why is that a problem?"

"Because Adderall and Ritalin are Schedule II controlled substances, and you're only supposed to be able to get them by prescription. Then a doctor can monitor you for weight loss or other complications and warn the hell out of you to stay away from alcohol while you're on the drug. If you buy the pills from a friend you don't get that support, and you can get into trouble."

My high school health teachers had done a good job of scaring me about drugs, and I'd only tried pot once or twice when I was in college, and nothing harder. I knew a couple of pre-med kids who got hold of amphetamines to help them study better, but I never tried them. And sure, I drank, but never to the point where it affected my life.

I pulled out a pad and began to make notes. "I know Eastern has been making strides in reducing alcohol on campus but I didn't know anything about Adderall or Ritalin."

"Once you get past those, the primary drug of choice is marijuana, which is to be expected in this population. College kids have been getting high for decades. Plus Eastern attracts students from around the country, many of them from places where marijuana has been decriminalized, so all they have to do is pack some weed in their bag to bring back for their friends after a trip home."

The server brought his salad and my sandwich, and I knew that Lili would be pleased that I had some vegetation in my meal. The only bad part was the bacon, and it was rare that I got to enjoy a whole sandwich without having to share some part of it with Rochester.

"But you want to hear about the arrest we made, and the kind of drugs he was selling," Tony said, after a couple of mouthfuls of salad. He wiped some dressing from his mouth. "Mr. Van Pool had a successful retail operation going based on fentanyl. You know what that is?"

"I've been learning."

"Have you learned yet that Pennsylvania is one of the states with the highest rates of opioid deaths? And I'm not just talking about

Philly and Pittsburgh. We have a couple of deaths every year here in Bucks County."

"Wow."

"We have determined that Mr. Van Pool ordered fentanyl online from China and had it sent to a mailbox franchise in Leighville, where he rented a large box. Then he'd break down the pills into small quantities and bottle them up. He had a high-quality printer in his room, and he'd print fake prescription labels in the name of the buyer."

"Smart kid," I said.

"Yeah, but you can never cover all your bases in an operation like that." He leaned forward. "The student who committed suicide, Tyler Benjamin?"

I nodded.

"His parents looked at the prescription bottles in his dorm room and insisted they hadn't come from his doctor. We figured out quickly that there was no doctor by that name, and the DEA number was fake. But we were stuck, until his mother finally closed down his PayPal account last month."

Tony knew how to tell a story. He stopped talking and started eating again, and I had to do the same and wait for him to continue.

"He had a record of payment to an email address his mother didn't recognize. It took us a while to track that address to Mr. Van Pool."

"Wow. So Earl Van Pool supplied Tyler Benjamin the drugs he used to commit suicide. Is that manslaughter?"

"We'd have to prove that Van Pool intentionally helped Benjamin kill himself. Which isn't going to happen. But we've got enough to charge him with illegal possession and intent to sell."

"You could subpoena Van Pool's PayPal account and see who else he sold to."

Tony frowned. "Who's the detective here? The one with years of experience at investigating cases?"

I resisted the urge to laugh, because he was right. It was the same argument I had with Rick when I overstepped my bounds. "That would be you."

"I can't tell you anything about the case that hasn't already been released. But yes, that would be an excellent next step in pursuing the case against Mr. Van Pool."

We finished eating, and I asked a few more questions about drug use on campus, and what Tony thought Eastern could do to protect students and detect problems. I wasn't naïve enough to think that was all we needed to do—Eastern had to protect its reputation, and President Babson would have a heart attack if we ever appeared in one of those party school listings.

"A lot of the time, you folks don't want to bring in law enforcement when you think you have a small problem on your hands," he said. "My advice is to involve us as soon as possible, because those small problems tend to be only the tip of the iceberg."

I paid for lunch, because I'd invited him, and we walked back out into the spring sunshine. It was hard to imagine all the dark stuff we'd been talking about when the sugar maples and hemlocks along Main Street were in bud, a robin darted between the branches in a flash of red, and students laughed with each other all around us.

I wondered how many of them held secrets, repressed fears, and self-medicated themselves so that they could put on that kind of happy front.

I couldn't tell from looking at any of them, but I knew that under the wrong kind of circumstances, any one of them could be at risk. It was up to me and my committee to do what we could to help them.

# Chapter 21
## *Symptoms of Abuse*

I drove directly from downtown Leighville up the hill to the campus and parked in the faculty lot. All around me, I saw evidence that spring was coming. Even though it was barely fifty degrees, a couple of boys in matching Kappa Sigma T-shirts wore shorts and tossed a ball back and forth with lacrosse rackets. The forsythia in front of Fields Hall had begun to bloom in bursts of brilliant yellow, and jonquils and iris were poking their light green shoots out of the flowerbeds along the pathways.

The Integrated Response Committee met in a conference room at the back of Fields Hall—what had once been the mansion's butler's pantry. The single conference table took up much of the room, and there wasn't a lot of space to swing your chair out.

"Sorry for the crummy room," Jackie Conrad said as she maneuvered herself into the armchair at the head of the table. "This must be a busy time for meetings because all the regular conference rooms are booked."

"It's actually not that," I said. "I have a counterpart at Friar Lake who runs the physical plant, and he reports to the VP of Operations. Apparently the College is renovating all the usual conference rooms with new carpet, furniture and light fixtures."

"All at the same time?" Ewan Garrett asked, his mouth open.

"Of course," Franklin Stone said. "That's the way we do things at Eastern."

"Well, *we* are charged with doing one thing differently," Jackie said. "Taking care of students who are so stressed that they might consider suicide. If we have to shake things up in order to save some lives, I want to do that."

I showed my PowerPoint on symptoms of student distress, and we all agreed that we had seen those to varying degrees. "But how do we determine what's serious and what's not?" Ewan Garrett asked.

"Experience," Franklin Stone said. "You see a hundred students with the same problem, you begin to understand the variations."

"What do you do without that range of experience, though?"

"How long ago did you finish your bachelor's?" Jackie Conrad asked Ewan.

"Six years ago."

"Then you go back to your experiences with friends and classmates," Jackie said. "You had a different angle on the problems, but you saw them, didn't you?"

Ewan nodded. "It's funny. I put so much effort into establishing a distance between me and the students, because I'm not much older than they are, but in this case I'm actually doing them a disservice."

"I want to add some information I learned at lunch today." I told them about meeting with Tony Rinaldi, and referred to my notepad to give them the statistics I'd learned.

Eve Kinsman, the coach, spoke up then. "I'm reluctant to involve the police when we can solve something at Eastern, without generating a criminal record for a student. Even a small charge can keep someone from a career in teaching or nursing or almost anything in medicine." She paused. "And it's bad publicity."

"It's a fine line," Jackie said. "And fortunately we don't have to walk it ourselves. All we have to do is make recommendations."

"I hope we can do more than that," Franklin Stone said. "If students are dying on my watch, I need to do something about it."

## Dog Willing

Coach Kinsman had put together an anonymous online survey for student athletes, asking them how they felt about the pressure to perform. She switched places with Jackie and put her presentation up on the screen. A pair of young women in Eastern cross-country uniforms laughed and hugged each other.

"In coaching, we want to encourage students to dig deep, to overcome obstacles, push through pain, and succeed, both on their own and as part of a team. All the research has shown that students who excel at athletics position themselves well for future success."

Her next photo was of a fit young man hunched over a laptop, and the despair was etched in his face.

"However, all the time and effort required to excel at college athletics puts very high demands on students. Their wins and losses are critiqued in the college newspaper, by their friends and classmates, and by the administration and alumni. Coaches can be terminated if their team doesn't display enough wins, and students know that. If they feel a bond to us, they feel an obligation to help us stay on."

She flipped to another screen, a bar chart. "I put together an anonymous survey and sent an invitation to every student who participates in intercollegiate athletics. The results were not surprising."

She pointed to the legend at the bottom of the screen. "My first question was about the level of stress students feel. As you can see, it's pretty high."

"I'll say," Ewan said. "Fifty-nine percent feel severe stress and another twenty-five percent extreme stress. What's the difference?"

"I categorized extreme stress as interfering with performance on or off the field. Paralyzing fear, nausea, that kind of thing. Severe stress is more like pressure to perform on behalf of the team, not to disappoint family and friends, and so on."

"I'll bet social media has something to do with that," Franklin Stone said. "I don't partake of it myself, but I hear students talking about Twitter and Instagram all the time, especially right after a big football or basketball game."

"That's true," Eve said. "The other coaches and I monitor the college accounts to cut out hurtful speech or negative comments. But we know that there is a lot of activity on personal accounts." She flipped to the next screen, which demonstrated what she had said. Students felt pressure from coaches, teammates, family members, and social media to perform, and were very upset when they received negative feedback.

She went through the rest of her survey results, and finally Ewan asked, "These are frightening numbers. How do we address them?"

"We have an advisor dedicated to student athletes," Eve said. "For the most part, though, he helps students choose courses that won't interfere with practice and travel schedules." She frowned. "My understanding is that he often directs them to gut courses like Rocks for Jocks or Physics for Poets."

Those were not the official names of those courses, but rather the informal ones. A student who needed a science course to meet core requirements could take one of those, which were notoriously easy.

"Are jock-sniffers still a phenomenon?" I asked Eve.

Jackie laughed. "I haven't heard that term in decades."

Eve frowned. "If you mean professors who favor athletes in their classes, and give them better grades simply because they can throw or catch a ball, then, yes. The students all know who those teachers are, or they can find them on Ratemyprofessor.com."

We brainstormed for a while, about how we could connect the advisor who focused on student athletes to the counseling system. "We could take a lot of the material you've put together and create a program for student-athletes about stress," I suggested. "We have a lot of open fields at Friar Lake. Perhaps you could organize a football or baseball team practice up there one day, and then afterwards we'd serve food and put on the presentation."

Eve agreed that might be a good idea, and we said we'd get together separately to frame it out.

"I keep going back to Tyler Benjamin," Ewan said. "If I had last semester to do over again, would any of what we are doing

## Dog Willing

have helped him? Because if not, then we're failing at our purpose."

"You said that you used discussion questions that came from the publisher in Tyler's class, didn't you?" I asked.

He nodded. I knew a lot of professors who did that—why reinvent the wheel, when a textbook author had already provided you with the materials you needed?

"One of our recommendations is going to be to customize at least a small part of many classes," I said. "If you knew last summer what you know now, you could have included a very pointed question in one of your quizzes, one that was designed to pick up on these problems. And then pick out any student who expressed despair, or suicidal tendencies, or opioid use."

"And then ask them each to come to your office hours for a consultation," Franklin Stone said. "If you're able to draw the student out about the problem, point out the appropriate resources."

"Maybe even walk the student over to the counseling office," Eve suggested.

"But what if they still won't tell us about their problems?" Ewan's voice was almost a wail, and I saw the pain he felt over Tyler Benjamin's suicide.

"Then you learn to move on," Jackie said gently. "None of us are trained as counselors. If a student doesn't want to reveal a problem to us then we grieve, and we move on."

On that note, we broke up.

On the way home I stopped at the drive-through pharmacy to pick up my regular blood pressure prescription—and so that Rochester could get one of the treats the pharmacy tech stockpiled for canine customers.

When we got home, I left the pills in their bag on the kitchen counter as I fixed dinner for Lili and me. Then I poured out some chow for the hound, and we all settled down to eat.

I told Lili about the meeting, and she added from her perspective in art that she'd like to get some training for her faculty about how to recognize danger signals in student art, and then how to address those.

As she stood up to begin clearing the dishes, Lili said, "I'm going back up to campus to meet with a couple of students I want to feature in the exhibition, to talk about how they want their work framed and hung. You and Rochester will be all right without me?"

"We can always amuse ourselves."

"And sometimes I worry about that," Lili said, but she kissed my cheek.

I handed her dishes from the table as she loaded the dishwasher, and once she had left for Eastern, I opened my laptop and added Lili's suggestion about including the art faculty to my own recommendations for the committee.

Then I opened my email program and discovered that Ramon had sent me the first five chapters of his novel. I'd already read the fifth, so I started with chapter one… and it seemed familiar. Had I already read that, too?

Then I realized that he was the author of the pages I had picked up at the food truck rally. A couple of the chapters, including that one, had been marked up electronically by Michael Wilmot's wife Amanda, which I could tell from the AW comments on the tracked changes.

Despite her own challenges, she was a good editor, and she had made a number of suggestions I agreed with. At the end, though, came the kicker. "This whole chapter, while including some lovely writing, doesn't relate to the main plot—the problems in medical billing at the doctor's office. I suggest you drop this and get right to the story."

I kept on reading, and after only a few pages I agreed with her. Chapter two began in the office, and while as a reader I appreciated a few of the details I had learned about the narrator when he and his wife went to a food truck rally, I didn't see that the first chapter related much to the rest of the book.

Ramon had clearly studied the basics of the thriller. By the end of chapter two, his protagonist, a billing clerk named Rafael Mena, had figured out that the practice was billing Medicare for long-dead patients. In the third chapter, he brought the problem up to the office manager, who criticized his abilities and indicated that he didn't seem to understand how the billing system worked.

"I can tell the difference between a dead patient and a live one," Rafael protested, but his boss ignored him. She was so carefully described that I felt sure he was describing a real woman, from her poorly colored red hair to the faux American Indian turquoise jewelry she wore.

Or he was very good at description. It was hard to tell.

By the end of chapter four, his hero had already received a death threat, and in the chapter I'd read with the group he was on the run.

That was where he had stalled, he wrote in his email to me. He didn't know where Rafael was going next, and until he did, he couldn't write any more. He blamed the group, and also the critique he had gotten from Nowak, for getting him stuck.

I was a pretty avid reader, and I had the idea that he had run out of steam for a couple of reasons. I wrote him an email and said how much I admired his writing, but that I had some ideas on how he could get moving again. I'd be happy to meet him for coffee sometime and share those, if he wanted.

I'd gone beyond looking for information from Ramon by then. He was floundering, jumping from medical billing to food trucks to novel-writing, and if I could give him a hand I wanted to.

I clicked "send," and stared at the screen. Would Ramon listen to my ideas? I wasn't a published writer or an editor or any of the gatekeepers in the publishing process. I was just an avid reader, particularly of detective and thriller fiction.

Then I heard a clatter and looked up. Rochester had his front paws up on the kitchen counter, as if he was looking for a treat, and he had knocked my pills to the floor.

I was about to complain to him, but then I remembered that he often used his nose, his head and his tail to send me messages—or at least that's the way I interpreted them.

"What's up, puppy?" I stood up, put the pills back on the counter, and gave him a green stick to chew. He went down on all fours, the stick in his mouth, and looked up at me. "Were you trying to tell me something? About my blood pressure?"

Statistics showed that you could lower your blood pressure by petting your dog or otherwise paying him attention. Was he saying he wasn't getting enough love?

I looked at the bottle of pills and remembered I'd been reading Ramon's story about medical office fraud. Did he have some experience with pills himself?

I put my hand under my chin, my finger over my lips, and thought about Ramon. The last time I'd seen him, he had been twitchy and agitated, and his boss, Otto, had complained he wasn't bathing regularly or paying attention to instructions.

All those symptoms clicked with what I had been learning about students, and others, using opioid drugs.

Was Ramon a user? Could he have taken his own fentanyl and sprinkled it over the croque monsieur he carried to Darlene Nowak?

Things started falling into place. He knew Darlene from both the food truck visits to her center and the critique group that had originally met at her store. He was angry about the comments she had made on his manuscript, and felt that her criticism had dried up his inspiration.

Add to that the possibility that if she created trouble for the food trucks, he might lose his job. I knew he had already lost all the money he had invested in training when the college where he was studying went out of business.

Could he have been a student at Liberty Bell University? Maybe he even knew Earl Van Pool, the pusher who had transferred from there to Eastern.

Was there a way to check a connection between them online? I opened a search engine and typed in "Earl Van Pool" and "Ramon Concepcion."

Immediately a result popped up. Both had signed a petition to both Pennsylvania Senators begging them to release Liberty Bell U students from their student loan debt.

Not only were they both students, the petition pages had been hand-signed, then scanned and uploaded, and Ramon's name was right beneath Earl's on the page.

Yeah, I knew that could be coincidence. Maybe they both happened to be on campus at the same time, flagged down one after another to sign the petition.

Or they knew each other and had been together when they ran into the person soliciting signatures.

None of the other search results were useful—they all omitted one term or another, and in one post Earl Van Pool had written about the opening scene of *The Umbrella Academy*, where a bunch of kids were born around the world in a kind of immaculate conception, where none of the moms had appeared pregnant before giving birth.

I tried Facebook and a couple of other social media sites. Were Ramon and Earl friends on any of them? No, but neither of them were very active users of any kind of social media.

That didn't make sense to me. Earl Van Pool was selling drugs. Surely he had to have an online profile? From what I understood, the drug business had migrated from shady characters on street corners to text messages and apps. Earl had to have a way people could get in touch with him, out there somewhere.

I climbed up to the attic and retrieved my hacker laptop to see if I could find anything that way. I knew that I was straying from one case, the death of Darlene Nowak, to another, the arrest of Earl Van Pool and his connection to Tyler Benjamin's suicide. But I had a hunch there was a connection somewhere, and I wondered if that connection was Ramon Concepcion.

# Chapter 22
## *Spoof*

My fingers tingled as I opened the laptop. I had promised both Rick and Lili that I wouldn't hack anywhere without letting one of them know, so there was that thrill of doing something potentially illicit along with the potential to betray my sweetheart and my best friend.

For a change, though, I had no idea where to start. I didn't know Earl's personal email address or his bank information, and I wasn't going to break in anywhere.

I heard Rochester chewing what sounded like paper somewhere in the house, and I got up to search for him. I carried the laptop with me until I found him on the bed, chewing the second page of an email Lili had printed out.

I took it out of his mouth and looked at it. There was nothing on the paper except the header information, including her address, lweinsto@eastern.edu.

That was an employee address – the first letter of the first name, then the first seven of the last name. My own was slevitan@eastern.edu, because I was lucky enough to have last name with only seven letters.

Students were formatted differently – and I realized that I could search for anything Earl Van Pool had done using his student mail address, which would have been vanpoole@students.eastern.edu.

I didn't imagine that he was dumb enough to use his student email address to make drug deals—but maybe he did something else with it. I sat on the bed beside Rochester and popped that into a specialized search engine that combed through the dark web, and sat back.

"Thanks for the clue, boy," I said, scratching Rochester under his neck, where he had a rich golden mane. "I know I can count on you when I'm stuck."

He gave me a doggie grin and rolled on his back. I rubbed his belly while the search engine scoured the dark web for me. I found only one good reference.

Someone on a message board had asked if anyone had done business with Earl's student email address, and another guy had responded that it was the same dealer as the one who used "separatelane" as an online ID.

I puzzled over that one for a minute until Rochester sat up beside me, assuming the position he usually took when we were riding in the car.

Of course. Van Pool was another name for carpool, and carpools got to ride in a separate lane on the highway. Though I didn't like the fact that Earl Van Pool was a drug dealer I was beginning to like his sense of humor.

Then I began to experiment with "separatelane" and a variety of different terms for opioids, including fentanyl. I got a lot of hits, people arranging drug deals with Earl Van Pool. Way more than I wanted to believe were taking place at Eastern College and in dead-in-the-sticks Leighville.

I didn't know what I could do with that information, though. I couldn't make a connection to Ramon Concepcion—he was probably using a different ID online. This was good evidence against Van Pool, though I knew from my experience with Rick I couldn't simply package it up and send it to Tony Rinaldi.

Lili pulled up in the driveway, and as I stowed the laptop away, Rochester rushed downstairs to bark at the front door until she came in. It was nearly eleven o'clock by then, time for Rochester's walk and bed. I grabbed a jacket and walked downstairs. I kissed Lili hello and asked how the gallery work had gone.

She pursed her lips and then kinked up one edge. "I'd love to refer at least two of these students for psychological counseling," she said. "But I keep reminding myself this is their creative work, and they're entitled to have an opinion, and a say in what's done. However when one girl said she wanted her photo framed with flecks of fourteen-karat-gold I had to gently remind her that she would be lucky if we used real wood in the frame rather than plastic."

I laughed. "I take it she didn't like that?"

"No, she most definitely did not. She said she'd ask her daddy for the money, and that was it. I'm afraid I spoke at a bit too much length about the appropriate way to frame student art, and the need for the exhibit to have some cohesion."

"Get it all off your chest," I laughed. "Then you won't need analysis or be tempted to take opioids to dull the pain of dealing with dull students."

She handed me Rochester's leash. "Go."

I laughed and hooked the dog up. Outside, as he paused to sniff a dogwood, I pulled out my phone and sent a text to Rick asking if we could meet for breakfast the next morning. I immediately got a response. "Why?"

"Question to ask you in person," I replied.

His response took a minute longer, and I watched as the three dots on my phone kept circling. "OMG," he finally wrote. "8:00 @ chocolate ear."

I sent back a smiling face.

Lili was already in bed by the time I returned with Rochester, so I stripped down and slid in beside her, and I was asleep in minutes.

My doggie alarm woke me at seven, as usual, by sniffing at my face, so that when I opened my eyes my field of vision was filled with a big black nose and dark brown eyes. Then he sealed the deal by licking my cheek.

I hurried him through the walk, then took a quick shower and dressed, and kissed a sleeping Lili goodbye.

Rick was sitting at one of the outdoor tables on Main Street as we walked up. Rochester rushed over, pulling me along like a water skier, and stuck his nose in Rick's crotch.

"I'll have a cappuccino and a chocolate croissant," Rick said. "And then you can tell me what's so urgent."

I left Rochester with him, and went into the café to fill his order and my own. The walls were painted a cheery yellow and had been complemented with Art Deco posters from French food companies, and it was always a warm and welcoming place. As Gail made Rick's cappuccino and a café mocha for me, I thought about Arielle's truck. Was she competing with Gail?

I doubted it. Sure, once every other week the trucks were in the shopping center on the other side of Main Street, but they were usually there in the afternoons or evenings, which were slow times for Gail anyway.

I remembered the bookstore, now closed. "Did you ever think of selling books here?" I asked Gail, as she handed me the coffees on a plastic tray.

"Maybe cookbooks," she said. "Or French knickknacks. The bookstore in the shopping center is closed, which doesn't bode well for that."

"From what I've seen, you have a lot more personal charm than the woman who owned it ever had," I said. "You could do open mic nights or host author readings, and that would bring in food and drink customers at slow times. Think about it. If you want some help choosing books I'd be glad to chime in."

She slid two chocolate croissants out of the warming oven and onto white china plates. "Thanks. I'll definitely let you know." She added one of her special biscuits for Rochester and then rang me up.

I carried the tray outside and set it on the table. I sat down and as

Rick reached for his cup I said, "I did a little searching on the deep web last night. Nothing illegal, you understand, but I'm not sure what to do with what I found."

I handed Rochester his biscuit, and he sat on the sidewalk and began chewing. I told Rick how I had tracked Earl Van Pool to a username called separatelane on one of the drug-related sites. "People have been using that site to set up drug deals with Van Pool."

"And?"

"How can I get that information to Tony Rinaldi? I don't want him to know about my – let's call them abilities. Even if I did tell him, would my evidence be enough to get a search warrant?"

"You could make an anonymous tip," Rick said. "Though I have to tell you those tips are often less than anonymous. If you use 911 to call it in, then they can track your number. I don't know what kind of software the Leighville PD online tip site uses, but ours strips out all identifying information before the text or the email comes to us."

He sipped his coffee. "However, there's still some varying degree of belief on the legal side if an anonymous tip is enough to justify a search warrant."

"What should I do?"

"If you provide enough information to substantiate the tip—for example, if you witnessed a traffic accident and gave specific details—then court precedent says that it's OK. But this is different. How would the police know if the source is credible enough?"

"They already know that Van Pool is dealing drugs," I said. "I'm just providing supporting evidence."

Rochester finished his biscuit and rolled over in the spring sunshine. An older couple passed us by on the way into the café, and I waited until they were gone.

"What if I spoofed an email address and sent everything to Tony that way?" I asked.

"I know what spoofing means—you're going to send it from an address that looks like it comes from someone else, right?"

I nodded.

"But how do you know Tony will see it and open it?"

"I'll send it from the chief of police. Or the mayor."

"Don't use his boss. Police chiefs tend to get touchy if someone messes with their identities."

He shrugged. "I guess it's a good way to get the information to him. You're sure that spoofing an address like that isn't illegal?"

"The focus on spoofing as a crime has been on phone numbers, rather than email addresses, and there are plenty of email forwarding sites that are perfectly legit. I'll be as careful as I can be."

Instead of heading directly to Friar Lake, I made a detour to Eastern. I left Rochester in the car with the windows open and hurried into the library, where I used one of the college computers to access the Internet and then get to my favorite email anonymizer with a .fi domain. For whatever reason, those Finns were among the first, and the best, at some legitimate address blocking.

I glanced around to make sure no one was watching me. Yeah, call me paranoid, but college kids can be nosy, especially if they see some old guy using a computer.

I looked up the mayor of Leighville's email address, and filled that in the "sender" field. Then I typed in as much information as I had about the way people had contacted Earl Van Pool through the dark web to buy fentanyl from him, including his separatelane ID.

Then I typed Tony's email address at the Leighville PD, hit send, and shut down the computer I'd been using. My pulse had been racing, and when I got back to the car I spent a moment or two petting Rochester, with his head on my lap.

When my pulse returned to normal, I gently nudged Rochester back onto his seat and drove up to Friar Lake. After getting some college work done, I checked my personal email and found a message from Ramon. He was eager to hear what I had to say about his book, because he was getting desperate to know where to take his book next. "I know it's going to take some time for Amazon royalties to land in my bank account, so the sooner I get this book finished the better."

There was another food truck rally at Pennsbury High the next day, he continued. Could I meet him earlier to go over my ideas?

I agreed. I spent most of the day trouble-shooting computer problems for a professional association of psychologists who had rented one of our classrooms. I only made it back to my office for a few minutes at lunch and then again in mid-afternoon to give Rochester some exercise.

Lili had lost her enthusiasm for the food trucks somewhere between the chilly weather, the flies that circled around the trucks, and the rickety tables and chairs, so she wished me luck that evening and said she'd make her own dinner.

That was okay with me; it meant I could drive directly from Friar Lake to Levittown and get to the rally before the trucks got too busy. I could have my conversation with Ramon, maybe get one of Michael's terrific cheese steak sandwiches, and then head for home.

At least, that was the plan.

# Chapter 23
## *Decal*

I got to the high school at five, under gray skies. The sound of the marching band practicing at the west campus floated through the air, reminding me of all those autumn nights when my friends and I gathered at this stadium, cheering for our team.

None of the food trucks had arrived yet, because they didn't start selling until six. I spotted a beat-up old Nissan sedan at the edge of the parking lot, and I pulled up beside it.

I let Rochester out of the car, and he immediately began sniffing around the grassy area. Then he went up on his front paws on the back of the Nissan, where he sniffed at a peeling Liberty Bell U parking decal.

That was further proof that Ramon had gone to the same school as Earl Van Pool. It wasn't an indictment, but it was a second sign, after the petition signatures, that he knew who Earl was. I took a picture of it, and the license plate, and texted it to Rick. I told him I was at the high school to talk to Ramon, and asked if he could find out if Ramon and Earl had been at school together.

Then I saw Ramon approaching from one of the porta-potties. "Thanks for coming out to meet me," he said. "I really want to hear what you have to say."

The football stadium was empty, so we walked over and sat on the first level of bleachers, in full view of anyone approaching the stadium area. "First of all, I agree with Amanda Wilmot that you started the story too early. You really don't need the first chapter."

"But I wanted to set him in his ordinary world," he said. "That's the first part of the hero's journey. Like Frodo in the Shire, before Gandalf shows up."

"I understand. But I think you're doing that pretty well in chapter two, when you introduce him at the office and show what he's doing. That's really his ordinary world, isn't it? The medical office, not the food trucks?"

"But I want to show that he has a wife he cares about."

"Then you can show a photo of her on his desk. Or he can talk to a co-worker about going to the food truck rally in a couple of sentences."

He nodded. "That sounds doable."

"I really like what you've written, but you're going very fast, and most of what you're writing is narration. You don't have very many actual scenes in these chapters. You could slow down, show him working, maybe have a conversation with his boss before he goes in to confront her. Right now she's really nasty, but real people have different shades. Maybe she's the one who stops by his desk to ask how his weekend was."

"She never cared about that stuff."

"She's your character," I said. "You can make her care. Or maybe she's being fake, asking nice questions of the people who work for her. Either way, you can show her behavior in a scene instead of Rafael telling us about her."

He opened his backpack and pulled out a notepad. "These are great ideas." He started scribbling, and I explained everything else I thought.

A chilly wind whistled down the gridiron, and I was sorry I'd left my sweater in the car, exposing my upper arms. Maybe I wouldn't stick around to get food after all, but head back to Stewart's Crossing and get something hot on the way.

"I want to go right home and get to work on this," he said. "But I have to work at Otto's truck first."

"I wanted to ask you a question," I said. "You went to Liberty Bell U, right?"

"Yeah, that's the place that screwed me over."

"Did you know a guy there named Earl Van Pool?"

Ramon's eyes narrowed. "Why do you want to know about Earl?"

"I work at Eastern College. He transferred there after Liberty Bell. He was apparently selling drugs to students, and I wondered if he was doing the same thing at his previous school."

He turned to his backpack and slid his notebook inside. Then it seemed like he was fiddling with something there. "I didn't know Earl very well. He was only in one class with me," he said, still focused on his backpack.

Rochester, who had been on the ground in front of us, rose up on all fours and barked.

"Oh, well, I was just curious." I stood up, and Ramon stood with me.

"Sometimes curiosity is a bad thing," Ramon said, and he turned back to me. I realized that he had a hypodermic needle in his hand.

Before I could move away, he had shoved it in my upper arm. Rochester began barking and growling furiously, but I couldn't say anything to him. I felt very fuzzy and my tongue was thick.

Then Ramon was pushing me down, between the bleachers, so I tumbled to the ground, hidden away from the world like a guy and his girl who wanted a secret place to make out. I'd done that once or twice myself, when I was a teenager who thought I could take any risk and live forever.

Then everything went black.

# Chapter 24
## *Final Response*

I woke up to someone calling my name. I looked up and saw Rick squatting beside me, gray light filtering between the bleachers above us. "It's OK, buddy," he said. "I gave you a shot that's going to counteract the drugs in your system."

In the background I heard the noise of an ambulance siren, and then there was a cluster of EMTs all around me. "Take care of the dog," I said, my voice scratchy.

"Always," Rick said.

Then I must have passed out again, because the next time I woke up I was in a hospital bed, with Lili beside me. "What happened?" I asked.

"You asked too many questions. As usual."

I struggled to sit up, but it was difficult because of all the tubes and wires in me.

"Stay there. It looks like somebody gave you a shot of some kind of narcotic drug and you passed out and fell behind the bleachers at the high school."

"Ramon," I said. "Fentanyl."

"That's what Rick thinks, too, but Ramon took off before the food truck rally started. Rick got a photo you sent him and decided to investigate himself. When he got to the high school Rochester was running around barking like a crazy dog, and as soon as Rick got out of his truck, Rochester led him over to you."

"My puppy," I said groggily.

"Rick noticed a spot of blood coming out of a puncture wound in your upper arm. It's lucky he had Narcan in his truck, and he was able to give you a shot while he waited for the ambulance." Her voice cracked. "Otherwise you might not have made it."

I reached one arm, stuck with tubes, out to her. "Wouldn't leave you," I said, and then I went to sleep again.

They kept me in the hospital overnight for observation because my blood pressure was running high, and then Lili took me home on Thursday morning. She took the day off to watch me for any further symptoms, but I was fine, if tired. I walked Rochester, napped, and read a book I was enjoying called *Cold Nose, Warm Heart,* a romantic comedy by Mara Wells, one of the Eastern English faculty.

I went back to work on Friday morning. I puttered around, answering emails, and discovered that Jackie Conrad had convened an emergency meeting of the Integrated Response Committee at one o'clock that afternoon. "President Babson has been called for comment on a story about drug dealing on campus," she wrote. "He wants to know what we suggest before he answers."

I accepted the meeting request without mentioning what I had learned about Earl Van Pool and Ramon Concepcion. I had been thinking about our committee during my enforced rest, and I had some ideas I wanted to research. By the time of the meeting, I had the numbers I needed.

The gray skies of the day before had fled, leaving behind a weak spring sunshine. I dropped Rochester at Lili's office and then walked over to Fields Hall. Since Ramon was only peripherally connected to our problem I decided not to mention my attack or my hospitalization to the committee. I wanted them to focus on what we could do for students.

I found the rest of the group in that small conference room and asked if I could make a brief presentation.

Everyone agreed, so I plugged my jump drive into the computer there, and pulled up the first slide. "I did some research and learned that the recommended ratio of students to counselors is one advisor per 250 students."

I flipped to the next. "As you know, at Eastern, advisors are assigned to students by their majors. The advisor who works with engineering and computer science majors is only responsible for fifty students, while the others have anywhere from three to five hundred."

"I didn't even know we had engineering courses," Ewan Garrett said.

"They're under Computer Science," I said. "Primarily they're intro courses for students who are interested in graduate study. There's one on chemical engineering for chemistry majors."

"And a bioengineering course for biology majors," Jackie added.

I looked at her. "We haven't been given a budget for this project, right?"

She smiled. "Of course not. Only a vague assurance from our beloved president that he'll make things work if we come up with some solid suggestions."

"Here's what I suggest, then," I said, and flipped to the next slide. "We ask to have the fifty students in computer science shifted over to the advisor who handles math and science students already. By the numbers, that's not a big deal, and it frees up a position for something new."

"Which is?" Franklin Stone asked.

I moved to the next slide, where I had created a quick flow chart. "Every single student referral by a faculty member goes to a new position, the advisor for integrated response."

A block figure with that title stood in the middle of my screen.

"That person reads the referral and contacts the student. The advisor does some digging to figure out what the student's base problem is and refers the student to the appropriate resources, then follows up."

I clicked a button and a bunch of arrows appeared moving from the advisor to the various resource departments.

"What do you mean by base problem?" Eve asked

"Let's say the student is missing assignments. Is that a problem with the material? The computer software? Maybe the student's mother is sick and he or she can't cope with schoolwork right now." I took a deep breath. "You know why we're having this emergency meeting, right? One of our students was arrested for dealing in fentanyl, and President Babson has to make a statement about drugs on campus."

"I heard a couple of my students talking about that," Garrett said. "But I don't know the details."

"Earl Van Pool, a science major, was arrested last weekend. He's been ordering fentanyl online from China, having it shipped to a mailbox in Leighville, then repackaging smaller numbers of pills with fake prescription labels."

The other members of the committee reacted with varying degrees of surprise, admiration and acknowledgment. "I can't tell you how I know, but I do know that some of his clients have been Eastern students – including Tyler Benjamin."

I let that sink in. "If President Babson agrees, I suggest that Eastern collect a list of Van Pool's clients from the police, and make them the first clients of this new advisor. The advisor can contact each one of them, and get them into the appropriate program, as well as deal with whatever underlying problem led them to opioids in the first place."

I flipped to my last screen, with a police photo of Earl Van Pool in the center. Arrows flowed back and forth between him and some imaginary student accounts.

"Drug abuse is a serious problem, and we can't simply brush these customers under the rug. I'd even suggest that we keep these students from either graduating or registering for the fall term until they meet with this advisor. I've looked at the student code of conduct and we have that leeway."

Jackie pushed her chair back. "That will be up to President Babson. I'm going to see if I can get him in here."

We talked amongst ourselves for a few minutes, until she returned and said, "We're moving to a bigger room."

She led us down the hall to the large room where the board of trustees usually met, adjacent to Babson's office. It had been the Fields family ballroom, and was festooned with plaster garlands above tall French doors that looked out at the rear garden.

President Babson was already there, accompanied by a dreadlocked black woman who was in charge of the college's public relations efforts.

"I understand your committee has an idea we can put forward to address the issue of a student dealing drugs on campus?" Babson asked.

Jackie looked at me. "This is your circus."

I took a deep breath. "Not exactly. What we're trying to do is get to the root of the problems students have, some of whom might resort to illegal substances to help them deal with what's going on in their lives."

I presented a brief summary of what the committee had been discussing, along with my PowerPoint, and Babson nodded at all the appropriate points. "I like it," he said finally. "It's a good way to shift the narrative away from the drug problem and focus more broadly on the issues that college students face, and how we're going to deal with them."

The committee worked with Babson and the PR director to create a statement about the upcoming changes, and as soon as we finished it, Babson emailed it directly to the TV reporter.

When I got home, I discovered a wicker basket in the courtyard with three items stuck into it. The first was a bottle of California chardonnay called Double Dog Dare. Alongside it was a square wooden plaque that read "Beware the Dog: He Will Steal Your Heart." And the most important, a box of special iced dog biscuits.

The card with it read, "From Arielle, Brandon, Sophia and Emma with love and pawprints for all your help." I carried it inside, put the wine in the refrigerator to chill, and gave Rochester one of the biscuits, which made him very happy.

I was pleased that Arielle had been released from suspicion, and I wondered how Otto felt about having employed a murderer.

Then I shivered. That situation was finished, out of my hands. Leave everything else up to the police.

That night, Lili and I watched the news in the living room with Rochester sprawled on the floor below us. Van Pool's activities were overshadowed by a crash on I-95, as a truck carrying a shipment of gourmet chocolates had collided with another delivering wine. Fortunately there was no loss of life, so the combination caused much merriment among the anchors, and the more serious news followed after the first commercial break.

As the news was finishing, Rochester rushed to the front door and began barking. I looked at Lili.

"Do you think Ramon tracked you down here?" she asked.

The memory hit me hard, falling beneath the bleachers, thinking that I had lost Lili and Rochester. I slumped down against the sofa. A man had tried to kill me—a man I hardly knew, one I had tried to help. I could have lost everything I had worked so hard to recover.

"Do you want me to call 911?" Lili reached for her cell phone.

With more surety in my voice than I believed, I said, "The security guards at the gate would have called."

Then I listened closely to Rochester. "That's his happy bark, not his warning growl." I leveraged myself up from the sofa and looked out through the courtyard. I spotted Rick's truck parked along the street, and the man himself striding up the driveway.

"It's Rick," I said, as I walked over to the door to let him in. Adrenaline flooded my body—not just to see my friend, but because there had been no threat. No need for that ancient fight or flight response.

"One of these days if no one else kills you, I will."

I turned to look at Lili, who had her arms crossed over her chest. "You take too many risks, Steve. For a smart man, you do dumb things. What if Rick hadn't gotten to you in time with that Narcan? What if the man who shot you last year had aimed better? What would I do if I lost you?"

She began to cry, and I started toward her but she shook her head. "Answer the damn door."

I was almost as glad to see Rick as Rochester was, though I resisted throwing myself at him and licking his hands. "I wanted to let you know as soon as I heard," he said, as he walked inside. "The Maryland State Police pulled over Ramon Concepcion on I-95 for driving erratically. They matched him to my outstanding warrant and detained him."

Lili had dried her eyes by then. "Thank you for telling us," she said.

He followed us into the living room, where he and Lili sat on sofa. "Are you all right?" he said to her.

She wiped an errant tear from her eye. "Fine. Happy to know he's in custody."

I stood over them. "Lili's not a big beer drinker, so you want me to open a bottle of wine?"

"I think that would be excellent," Rick said, still looking at Lili.

I opened the bottle of Double Dog Dare chardonnay and poured us three glasses.

"Here's to Narcan," I said, holding my glass up. "And good friends who carry it with them."

We tipped our glasses together. "Did Ramon say where he was going when he was arrested?" I asked.

"He was apparently trying to drive to Key West, where he hoped to get on a boat to Cuba."

"Do you think he killed Darlene Nowak?"

"He as much as admitted it. That she had been rude to him, criticized his writing, made him think that he was going to fail at that like everything else in his life. When you asked him about the drug dealer at Eastern, he realized that you could connect him to fentanyl, and that meant he'd move up on the suspect list."

"So he tried to kill me?"

My hand began to shake, and I put my wine glass down on the coffee table.

"And he would have, if you hadn't texted me. He had a whole bunch of pharmaceutical supplies in his backpack, left over from the school he dropped out of. He had been planning to use the hypodermic with fentanyl in it on his boss at the food truck the next time the guy bitched at him, but he decided to use it on you instead."

"I'm sure Otto will be grateful."

"You never should have gone to that rally alone," Rick said.

I nodded. "I thought there'd be more people there, setting up. I didn't realize the area would be empty. And I wasn't thinking about Ramon as a possible killer, even though I knew about the connection between him and Earl Van Pool." I shrugged. "I thought I could help him with his writing."

"In the future, save the teaching for the college, where they pay you for it, all right?" he asked. "You do your job, and I'll do mine."

"I'm not teaching this semester."

"Whatever. You know what I mean."

I nodded.

"His head is pretty hard," Lili said. "Maybe the next time he gets in trouble someone will knock some sense into it."

Rick laughed, and I followed, and soon all three of us were smiling. "Not to say there's going to be a next time," I said, but I was glad that Lili and Rick would support me if there was.

∽

*Dog Willing*

Saturday morning, Gail Dukowski emailed me to ask if I'd help her choose some books to offer for sale at the Chocolate Ear, and I agreed quickly. Later that morning, I took Rochester down there, and left him in the dog-friendly annex while I spoke to her.

"Now that Book Crossing is out of business, I can see that there's an opportunity to sell some books along with gifts and crafts here at the café. But there are so many to choose from—I was hoping you could help me curate a list."

"I'd love to."

She handed me a couple of print catalogs. "Why don't we sit over in the annex and go through these? I'll bring a café mocha and a chocolate croissant for you, and a biscuit for Rochester."

"You know us so well."

"That's the advantage to living in a small town, getting to know your customers."

We spent the next hour browsing through print and online catalogs, choosing a bunch of dog-related books for the annex, like the Pampered Pets series by Sparkle Abbey and the Chet and Bernie mysteries by Spencer Quinn. We also chose some cookbooks and French gift items for the café. As we were finishing, Arielle Brodeur came in. I saw her son and daughter in the café through the glass door that connected the two rooms.

"Steve! I'm so glad to see you. I can't thank you enough for what you did for me."

I stood up, and we hugged, and she kissed me on each cheek in the French way. I introduced her to Gail. "I was hoping to talk to you," Arielle said. "I've been running a French food truck."

"I know. I had one of your *croque monsieurs* the last time you were here. It was terrific."

Arielle smiled. "Thank you. Part of the fallout from the bookstore owner's murder is that the police had a long talk with my assistant, Keenwa. They aren't going to prosecute her for a crime she was involved in, as long as she goes back to school full time. So I'm going to cut back on food truck rallies."

She looked at Gail shyly. "Something Steve said triggered an idea in my head, and I've been looking at your menu. Most of your offerings are sweet, aren't they, rather than savory?"

Gail nodded.

"I was wondering if I could prepare some savory items for you as an experiment. Perhaps for later in the day?"

"I'd love to see what you can offer," Gail said. "Why don't you put together a selection you think might work, and we'll have a tasting one day?"

Arielle turned to me. "You'll have to come, too. With Lili. And I'm supposed to tell you from Otto and all the other vendors, any time you want to come to a rally you guys eat free, in thanks for all you've done for all of us."

"That's very kind of you," I said.

Gail stood up. "I need to head next door and serve some customers. But leave me your card, Arielle, and we'll set something up."

She ducked into the café, and I said, "I'm really pleased things have worked out for you. Are you going to be able to stay in River Bend?"

"I am. Pierre and I have had a couple of very long talks, and we're both committed to doing what's best for the kids. If I can, I'm going to transition toward supplying stores like this one with pastry rather than selling myself. That will give me a lot more flexibility." She smiled. "Pierre's even volunteered to help. So I think we'll be staying in place for a while."

"That's great." Rochester sat up on his haunches then and sniffed Arielle's hand, and she petted him. "Rochester will be happy to continue his romance with Emma."

Arielle went next door to pay for her kids' selections, and I rubbed Rochester under his neck. "Another successful investigation, huh boy?"

He woofed once in agreement.

# Thanks for reading!

Thanks for reading! There's another Golden Retriever Mystery in the pipeline—*Dog's Waiting Room*. You can hear about it when it's ready through my newsletter or Facebook page.

I'd love to stay in touch with you. Subscribe to one or more of my newsletters: Gay Mystery and Romance or Golden Retriever Mysteries and I promise I won't spam you!

Follow me at Goodreads to see what I'm reading, and my author page at Facebook where I post news and giveaways.

If you liked this book, please consider posting a brief review at your vendor, at Goodreads and in reader groups. Even a short review help other readers discover books they might like. Thanks!

Here is the series in order:

1. In Dog We Trust
2. Kingdom of Dog
3. Dog Helps Those
4. Dog Bless You
5. Whom Dog Hath Joined
6. Dog Have Mercy

*Thanks for reading!*

7. Honest to Dog
8. Dog is in the Details
9. Dog Knows
10. Dog's Green Earth
11. A Litter of Golden Mysteries

# Acknowledgments

*Cold Nose, Warm Heart* is a real book by a Broward College colleague of mine who uses the pen name Mara Wells. The Pampered Pets series of cozy mysteries is also a lot of fun for pet lovers. And even though I'm not a fan of talking dogs, I've really enjoyed Chet the Jet, the failed police dog who narrates those books.

The BookBitch™ is a trademark used by Stacy Alesi, an excellent reviewer of mystery books. Nothing in this work of fiction should be construed to resemble her, or any other member of the mystery community. No booksellers were harmed in the writing or research of this book.

I would like to acknowledge the support of my colleagues at Broward College, and my fellow members of Mystery Writers of America. And of course my husband Marc and our golden retrievers, Brody and Griffin, who continue to inspire me with their antics.

www.ingramcontent.com/pod-product-compliance
Lightning Source LLC
LaVergne TN
LVHW012016060526
838201LV00061B/4339